Now &
Always

clearwater crossing

Now & Always

laura peyton roberts

BANTAM BOOKS
NEW YORK • TORONTO • LONDON • SYDNEY • AUCKLAND

RL 5.8, age 12 and up
NOW & ALWAYS
A Bantam Book/August 2001

ISBN 0-553-49378-7

Visit us on the Web! www.randomhouse.com/teens
Educators and librarians, for a variety of teaching tools, visit us at
www.randomhouse.com/teachers

Published simultaneously in the United States and Canada

Bantam Books is an imprint of Random House Children's Books, a
division of Random House, Inc. BANTAM BOOKS and the rooster
colophon are registered trademarks of Random House, Inc.
Bantam Books, 1540 Broadway, New York, New York 10036.

PRINTED IN THE UNITED STATES OF AMERICA

OPM 10 9 8 7 6 5 4 3 2 1

If I speak in the tongues of men and of angels, but have not love, I am only a resounding gong or a clanging cymbal. If I have the gift of prophecy and can fathom all mysteries and all knowledge, and if I have a faith that can move mountains, but have not love, I am nothing. If I give all I possess to the poor and surrender my body to the flames, but have not love, I gain nothing.

Love is patient, love is kind. It does not envy, it does not boast, it is not proud. It is not rude, it is not self-seeking, it is not easily angered, it keeps no record of wrongs. Love does not delight in evil but rejoices with the truth. It always protects, always trusts, always hopes, always perseveres.

Love never fails. But where there are prophecies, they will cease; where there are tongues, they will be stilled; where there is knowledge, it will pass away. For we know in part and we prophesy in part, but when perfection comes, the imperfect disappears. When I was a child, I talked like a child, I thought like a child, I reasoned like a child. When I became a man, I put childish ways behind me. Now we see but a poor reflection as in a mirror; then we shall see face to face. Now I know in part; then I shall know fully, even as I am fully known.

And now these three remain: faith, hope and love. But the greatest of these is love.

1 Corinthians 13:1–13

One

"You're *sure* you'll be all right by yourself?" Mrs. Rosenthal asked Leah. Mother and daughter were standing on the sidewalk in front of their condominium building Saturday morning, handing Mr. Rosenthal bags and suitcases to put in the trunk of his Ford sedan. "Two weeks is a long time and if you even *think* you're going to be scared—"

"I'll be *fine*," Leah said automatically. She'd already repeated it so many times she'd lost count. "Anyway, you're going to Arkansas, not the Arctic. Not that you don't have the luggage for it," she added with an amused lift of one eyebrow.

Her father shook his head as he rearranged things in the trunk, trying to make more room. "No kidding, Arlene. I thought this was supposed to be a shopping trip, but you've already filled up the car."

"You have our itinerary," Leah's mother said, ignoring her husband. "If you need us for anything, anything at all, then—"

"Figure it out by yourself," Mr. Rosenthal advised. "Don't call us unless the place burns down."

1

"Joseph!" his wife objected.

"Leah knows I'm kidding." Stuffing the last bag into place, Mr. Rosenthal slammed the trunk. "If you don't want to miss the bus, we'd better get going."

Leah's parents had signed up for a two-week tour through Arkansas and Tennessee, stopping at bed-and-breakfasts and numerous small antique shops along the way. Mr. Rosenthal hadn't been particularly excited by his wife's choice of activity, and Mrs. Rosenthal had been desperate to include Leah, but in the end they had decided to go alone, Leah being equally determined to stay behind in Clearwater Crossing with her boyfriend, Miguel del Rios. She was still amazed that her parents had actually agreed to let her, but here they were, all packed up, ready to go meet the tour group in Harrison.

"It's not too late to change your mind," her mother offered with a catch in her voice. "There's always one more seat on a bus."

The words tugged at Leah's heart. As much as she had wanted to stay behind, there was no denying that part of her was sorry now, wishing she were going. The trip was sounding more fun all the time, and she was definitely going to miss her parents. And then there was the whole question of being alone and unsupervised with Miguel. Night after night after night . . .

It's almost too much pressure, she thought, wishing

2

she could turn back the clock a year. *It would be so great to be starting senior year at CCHS with Miguel in the fall, to have all that time together stretching out before us.*

Instead they were down to a few last weeks before Leah left for Stanford in California and Miguel started classes at Clearwater University. Just a few last weeks to cram in all the things they hadn't done yet. *All* the things.

Ready or not . . . , she thought nervously.

She was actually on the verge of running inside to pack a suitcase when her father stepped forward and gave her a reassuring hug.

"Pay no attention to your mother," he said. "You'll be fine. *She's* the one I'm worried about." He had barely been able to convince his wife to go without Leah in the first place, and in the week that had passed since she'd made the tour reservations, she had threatened to cancel at least once a day. In the end Mr. Rosenthal had prevailed, though, and now he stood dangling his car keys, itching to be on the road.

"We trust you," her mother said for the millionth time, squeezing Leah nearly breathless. "You take care of yourself."

The next thing Leah knew, she was waving to the back of the Ford.

They were gone. She was alone.

Two whole weeks.

I should call Miguel and see if he wants to come over now.

She knew he would be home, working on one of his many projects at the ancient two-story house his family had bought and moved into a week before. They were all incredibly happy but still living mostly out of boxes, not wanting to unpack things they'd only have to move again in the course of renovation. According to Miguel, every surface in the building needed to be sanded, or painted, or varnished. Anyone could see they needed to be cleaned.

Or maybe I'll just go over there and help him.

After all, they were going to have two whole weeks of alone-time together.

They might as well pace themselves.

"Stop bolting your food, Benny," Mrs. Pipkin said, scowling. "It's bad for your digestion."

The Pipkin family was seated around the kitchen table, even though Ben had tried to get out of lunch by saying he wasn't hungry. Ben flashed his mother a weak smile and took another, smaller bite of his tuna sandwich, chewing faster to make up for it. He was in an excruciating hurry, but he didn't want his parents to know that.

"More potato chips?" his father offered, holding out the bag.

4

Ben shook his head, eager to finish and be on his way.

"Why not?" his mother asked suspiciously. "What's the rush?"

"No rush," he said quickly.

The truth was that he was meeting Bernie Carter at the arcade and he had the entire encounter planned down to the minute: Meet Bernie at one-thirty, play games until three o'clock, and eat ice cream bars at that new dip-your-own place immediately after that. If everything stayed on schedule, he'd still have time to walk Bernie home by four, when she was supposed to start baby-sitting her younger brother, Elton, while their mother went to work. The last thing Ben wanted was for *his* mother to start asking a lot of time-consuming questions and ruin his delicate timing.

The last thing Ben wanted was for his mother to start asking a lot of questions.

It was bad enough that everyone in Eight Prime knew about Bernie now, courtesy of Miguel's and Leah's big mouths. Ben didn't mind being ribbed about having a girlfriend—actually, he kind of liked that part—but for the past week he had lived in constant fear that one of his friends would run into Bernie by herself somewhere and say terrible things about him. Like the truth. Somehow, by some miracle, Bernie was under the impression that Ben was cool. Seven-year-old Elton liked Ben, and apparently that was good enough for Bernie. The fact that a seven-year-old might not be the best judge of cool apparently hadn't occurred to her.

Ben was praying it never would.

"Are you seeing that Bernie girl again? I want to meet her," Ben's mother announced.

Ben sucked a hunk of sandwich down his windpipe. His mother? And Bernie? Together?

"Wh-what?" he gasped, still choking.

"The arcade is a waste of money anyway, especially when your father has more computer games here than they do. Why don't you bring your little friend to the house instead?"

That's why, Ben thought frantically. The mere fact that his mother could refer to Bernie as his "little friend" would have been reason enough. But in truth, her unfortunate way with words was barely the tip of the iceberg.

"No! I mean, uh, we already planned on the arcade." Ben checked his watch, desperate for any excuse. "In fact, she's probably already on her way there. I'd better leave right now."

He jumped up from the table and ran to brush his teeth, ignoring his mother's protests that he hadn't finished his lunch. He knew she'd finish it for him. She always did.

Ever since Ben was little, his mother had been overweight. Even in elementary school it had embarrassed him, but as she'd continued to pack on the

6

pounds, year after year, he had started devising strategies to make sure people from school never saw them together. Ironically, the fatter she got, the easier it got to hide her. She was so heavy now that she could barely get up from a chair by herself; she rarely left the house except to go to the grocery store.

And if her weight wasn't bad enough, she spoke to him as if he were still five. No matter how he begged, he couldn't break her of calling him Benny, referring to him as a boy, or making loud, incredibly embarrassing comments on those rare occasions when they did venture out in public.

"Eat more salad, Benny," she'd advise in a restaurant. "A growing boy needs to stay regular." Or, at the department store, "What do you want with pants that hang halfway off your bottom? Those are going to chafe your crotch."

His father was a different story. A total computer geek, right down to the glasses and pocket protector, Mr. Pipkin had an almost legendary unawareness of his personal appearance, to the point that he had once absentmindedly worn his wife's pink bathrobe to work. Ben had only recently learned to appreciate the man's genius enough to overlook his fashion sense—which still didn't mean he was in a hurry to invite his friends over to meet him. Not everyone thought software engineers were cool.

"I'm leaving!" Ben called from the entryway,

slamming the front door before anyone could tell him different.

A cute, funny, totally amazing girl like Bernie could easily find someone much cooler than Ben to go out with. It wouldn't even be a challenge. The challenge was keeping her thinking that Ben was the smart, sophisticated older guy she'd been looking for, instead of the geek he was.

One minute with his parents and any chance of maintaining that illusion would be all over. Once Humpty Dumpty fell off *that* wall, they'd never put the pieces together again.

"This one is good," Jenna Conrad murmured intently, reaching for her scissors. "Except for that ugly striped ribbon. What's the story with that?"

She cut the photograph of a bridesmaid's bouquet from one of the many magazines stacked carefully on her twin bed and then picked up a pen. REPLACE WITH WHITE OR PASTEL RIBBON, she printed neatly across the bottom, drawing an arrow pointing to the offending bow.

"Sometimes these designers get so carried away...," she muttered, trimming the edges perfectly square before adding the clipping to the growing pile on her nightstand.

The CD she'd been listening to came to an end. Jenna jumped up to put in a new one, accidentally scattering magazines everywhere.

"Great!" she exclaimed, hands on hips. "I had all those in order!"

Swapping discs impatiently, she hurried back to her project. She had purchased new issues of all the bridal magazines earlier that Saturday, and that meant that the old issues needed to be relieved of their useful parts and disposed of. Not that Jenna's older sister, Caitlin, understood that.

"Why can't we just stick them in the bookshelf instead of cutting them up?" she'd asked. "Then, after I'm married, we'll throw them all out."

"Because you can't *see* anything that way," Jenna had explained. "You can't *compare* anything. You can't even find where things are!"

"I thought you had everything bookmarked," Caitlin had said dubiously.

That wasn't the point, but Jenna hadn't had time to make Caitlin understand the importance of her system before David Altmann had shown up and whisked his fiancée off to the movies.

"I still can't believe she went," Jenna grumbled now. After all, once Caitlin and David were married, they were going to see each other every day for the rest of their lives. She and Caitlin only had five weeks to plan the wedding.

Which is total insanity, Jenna thought, zeroing in on a cake that might work and reaching for the scissors again. *Who ever heard of planning a wedding in five weeks?*

As pleased as both the Conrads and Altmanns were about the impending wedding, no one was especially thrilled that the date had been set so soon. No one except Caitlin and David, anyway. But David had been offered a job in Chicago beginning in September, and the choices were for Caitlin to stay behind in Clearwater Crossing, planning a fancy wedding for later in the year, or to wed less elaborately now in order to go to Chicago with David as his wife. No one even considered that Caitlin might go to Chicago before she was married, and the fact that the church and all the popular reception sites had been spoken for for months didn't deter her in the least.

"What difference do the details make, so long as we have a wedding?" she'd declared, her cheeks flushed with passion. "If we have to, we'll hold the ceremony on a Tuesday and have the reception in our backyard."

Jenna had nearly fainted at the thought. On a Tuesday? Not in *her* backyard!

Luckily it helped to have connections. Even though their church had already been booked with the maximum two weddings on Saturday, August twenty-first, Mrs. Conrad had managed to get special permission to squeeze Caitlin's in at ten in the morning. It was a lot earlier than Jenna would have liked, but still . . . Being the choir director obviously counted for something. The reception site remained up in the air, though. Every good restaurant was already booked. There had been some talk of using the church hall, but that was taken too.

"I hope those two are at least coming up with a guest list tonight," Jenna muttered, going for the scissors again, then changing her mind. She didn't like that dress after all. "It's kind of hard planning a reception when you don't even know how many people are coming!"

She dropped the first gutted magazine off the side of her bed and was reaching for another when a new song on the CD made her stop and listen.

"This one's good," she said, reaching for a pad and pen to jot down its title. The band she'd just joined, Trinity, was going to play at Caitlin's reception, and they were scrambling like crazy to make sure they were ready in time. They needed to learn a bunch more songs, and even then they might have to resort to playing CDs at least part of the time. All four members of the band—Guy Vaughn, Jenna, Evan, and Paul—were swapping every CD they owned in an attempt to come up with a final playlist.

Jenna picked up a second magazine, then changed her mind and dropped it in favor of the pad again. Thinking about songs reminded her that she still hadn't finished the lyrics for the one she was writing for Caitlin and David. Guy was going to set it to music for her, but she had to give him something to work with.

There's just too much to do! Who can keep track of it all? she thought, flipping backward through her steno pad. She was still working on her idea of lifting a passage from the Bible and simply rearranging it a bit, and somewhere in all that scribbling she had copied out a bunch of promising verses.

"Jenna!" Mrs. Conrad called up the stairs to Jenna's third-floor room. "Can you come down to the landing?"

Pausing the CD player, Jenna ran down in her socks. "Yeah, Mom?"

"Did Caitlin happen to tell you when she wants to go shopping for dresses? Did she get Monday off from Dr. Campbell?"

"She didn't say," Jenna replied, annoyed that she hadn't thought to ask. If they were going shopping on Monday, Jenna needed to take a day off from her counselor duties at the Junior Explorers' summer day camp, which meant she needed to let Peter know to plan around her absence. "I'll ask her the minute she gets home," Jenna promised, running back up to her room.

How are we ever going to get everything done in time? Especially with Caitlin taking such a laid-back attitude? People could try to help her, but if she wasn't around to make the final decisions, nothing was ever going to get planned!

I wish I were making the final decisions, Jenna admitted to herself. She could never say that out loud,

12

of course, especially not to Caitlin, but things would go so much more smoothly if she were the one in charge. She'd already practically memorized the bridal planner, and Cat had barely glanced at it. She knew exactly how every dress should look, what flavor of cake tasted best, and who ought to arrange the flowers. Caitlin hadn't even picked her colors!

If this were my wedding, I'd be so on top of everything. If I only had five weeks to plan, I wouldn't sleep until the honeymoon!

Jenna forced herself to take a deep breath.

No point getting worked up. When Caitlin gets home, I'll just go through the calendar with her. I don't care if it takes us all night. When she sees how little time is left, she'll have to get with the program!

Two

"Don't tell me you're still sleeping!" Courtney Bell's familiar voice teased over the telephone. "Shouldn't you be at church or something?"

"If you really thought I was at church, then why are you calling me?" Nicole retorted grouchily, rolling over in bed to check the clock on her nightstand—ten. Her family must have gone to services without her again, the only welcome pattern to emerge from the last few weeks of fighting about the baby Mrs. Brewster was going to have. Nicole swung her bare feet down to the floor and tried to clear her muddled head.

"I assume you're back from your retreat," she said, managing not to sound nearly as glad as she was. Courtney had been gone for two whole weeks on some stupid, tree-hugging adventure of self-discovery. Not only had she given Nicole practically no advance warning, they hadn't even had telephones where she'd gone.

"That's right! So drag your butt out of bed. I'll be there in fifteen minutes."

14

"Courtney!" Nicole protested. "I just woke up. I haven't showered, or dressed, or eaten, or any—"

"Okay. See you in ten. Have I got a surprise for you!"

"What kind of surprise?" Nicole asked suspiciously, but the phone had already gone dead. "Great," she muttered, running for the bathroom.

She hesitated in front of the scale a moment, then hurried past it into the shower instead. *Courtney didn't leave me time to weigh myself*, she thought by way of excuse.

Not that she particularly wanted to see the damage from the hot fudge sundae she'd eaten the night before. Her weight had been gradually creeping up all summer, ever since she'd gone on that weeklong eating binge at cheerleading camp. She had gained ten pounds overall—and for all she knew it was eleven now. She had tried a bunch of different diets, but the weight just didn't fall off anymore, not the way it had when she'd started dieting the previous summer. Even though she was still a lot lighter than she'd been back then, Nicole had recently become convinced that something was wrong with her metabolism. Instead of the self-control she'd prided herself on for the past year, now she felt out of control. All she ever thought about was food, food, food.

Well, food and Noel.

The fact that Nicole had put on some weight definitely hadn't been lost on her hot new boyfriend. He

15

was constantly making cracks about fat girls, then looking at her to see if she got the connection. She got it, all right. She got it loud and clear. But so far she hadn't seemed able to do too much about it.

If only Mom wasn't having a baby! she thought, reaching for the shampoo as the water pelted down on her head. The stress of that unwelcome development had to be at least part of the reason she couldn't stop eating. Nicole had known about her new sibling for a few weeks now, although none of them knew whether it was a boy or a girl. As if waiting until nearly November for it to be born wasn't enough suspense, Nicole's parents had decided they wanted to be surprised by the sex.

At their age, having a baby ought to be surprise enough. It certainly was for Nicole. And even though she was getting used to the idea, she still didn't like it much.

She turned off the water right as the doorbell rang.

"Already?" she exclaimed, reaching for a towel. "What's Courtney's hurry?"

Although now that she was awake, Nicole had to admit she was excited about seeing her best friend again. It had been hard having her away for two whole weeks, especially since no one else had known about the baby when Courtney left. Nicole had been too embarrassed by the whole situation to tell any of her other friends. But in the week since she'd finally told Jenna—who had been thrilled—Nicole had gradually found the courage to inform the rest of Eight Prime. If they weren't all as enraptured as Jenna at the thought of a baby, at least no one seemed to think it was bad news.

An impatient pounding on the front door sent Nicole scurrying for her bathrobe, hair still uncombed and dripping onto her shoulders.

"I'm coming, I'm coming," she muttered, charging down the stairs without even a hint of makeup on.

If Court's determined to get here so early, she has to take what she gets, she thought, pulling the front door open. At the sight of the duo on her doorstep, though, Nicole froze in her tracks, forgetting even to breathe. One of the girls was Courtney, her trademark red hair wound into a curly puff on top of her head. But the other . . .

"Gail!" Nicole gasped, stunned to be face to face with the cousin who hadn't spoken to her for months, not since Nicole had unwittingly gotten them both emancipated from fast-food slavery at Wienerageous. Gail looked different—her previously jet-black hair was now streaked with red and cut blunt at her chin, and her once milky skin had obviously seen the sun that summer. Her wide blue eyes hadn't changed, though. Nicole remembered well how quickly they could shift from completely innocent to something entirely different.

17

"Happy to see me?" Gail asked, a spark of mischief lurking in those eyes now. "Love the robe, by the way. Very stylish."

Nicole glanced down self-consciously, painfully aware that her thick chenille bathrobe made her look like a powder-blue sausage. Courtney and Gail, on the other hand, were enviably long and lean in practically identical outfits of shorts, tight tank tops, and black platform sandals.

"Aren't you going to invite us in?" Courtney asked, brushing past into the entryway.

Nicole just stood staring at Gail, still unable to understand why her cousin was there. Gail and Courtney didn't even know each other. And then there was the whole not-speaking-to-her part. The last time Nicole had talked to her cousin, Gail had been in hysterics about Nicole's getting her fired from her job and forbidden from seeing her college-age boyfriend, Neil. The fact that Nicole had also saved her from the advances of their lecherous thirty-four-year-old boss had somehow gotten lost amid the tears and recriminations.

"What are you doing with Courtney?" Nicole finally asked. She could hear her best friend banging around in the kitchen, helping herself to something to eat. "How did you two meet?"

"At the retreat, of course," Gail replied, giving up on an invitation and walking inside as well.

"She heard my last name was Brewster, and it didn't take rocket science to put things together from there."

"I'm scooping ice cream!" Courtney called from the kitchen.

"For breakfast?" Nicole hurried to check on her friend, leaving Gail to follow. Courtney already had three bowls set out, which she was filling from a half gallon of rocky road.

"It's practically lunch for *some* people," Courtney retorted. "But if ice cream isn't on your diet, I'll understand if you eat celery instead."

"Yeah. Put on a few, haven't you, cuz?" Gail asked, looking her up and down.

"No!" Nicole lied, certain that the pounds she had gained since she'd last seen her cousin would be invisible under the bathrobe.

"That's not what I heard," said Gail, exchanging a knowing look with Courtney.

"You guys were talking about me?" Nicole bleated.

"Unless you like exploring your touchy-feely side and jumping out of trees, there wasn't a lot else to do at that stupid retreat." Gail flipped her multicolored hair. "I wouldn't even have gone if my parents hadn't made me. Like two weeks in Dullsville is going to make me forget about Doug!"

Courtney grinned appreciatively and began putting second scoops in the bowls.

"What are you smiling about?" Nicole asked her. "You're the one who was so hot on going!"

Courtney polished off the carton and dropped it into the trash. "That was all a phase. I'm over it now."

"What do you mean, all a phase?" Nicole demanded. "You sound like Dorothy, waking up from Oz."

Gail cackled and pointed her spoon at Courtney. "I'll get you, my pretty!" she mimicked, an expert witch. "And your little dog, too."

Courtney howled with laughter while Nicole silently wondered if she was supposed to be the dog. She certainly *felt* like the dog.

"And who's Doug?" Nicole asked Gail, abrupt in her confusion. "I thought you were so in love with Neil."

Gail rolled her eyes. "Too many boys, too little time," she said dismissively. "Neil had me long enough."

Courtney laughed again; Gail was obviously her new idol. "You're not kidding! I can't believe I let stupid Kyle Snowden depress me so long. Like I care what he thinks! Hurry up and eat, Nicole. As soon as you get dressed, we're going to the mall to find me a new boyfriend."

"Maybe at The Gap," Gail said. "I saw a couple I liked in their last TV ad."

The pair of them ran through some lengthy hand-slapping thing they'd apparently learned at camp.

Nicole sat down hard and began shoveling rocky road into her mouth. She had every intention of breaking her recent ice cream–eating habit, but that would have to wait until tomorrow. She had bigger things to worry about just then—such as whether she liked the idea of Courtney and Gail being so buddy-buddy, whether Gail had forgiven her for what happened at Wienerageous, and what Mrs. Brewster was going to say when she got home from church and found the three of them polishing off her ice cream.

"Eating for two now, huh, Nicole?" Gail teased. "Oh, wait. That's your mother."

Courtney laughed so hard she nearly choked. Tears squeezed from her closed green eyes and the curls bounced on her head.

"You are so *funny!*" she gasped, slapping Gail's arm. "How come you never told me your cousin was so funny?" she asked Nicole.

"Well . . . I . . . ," Nicole began.

Gail leaned back in her chair, her eyes fixed on Nicole's. "There are *lots* of things my cousin doesn't know about me."

"Peter!" Mrs. Altmann called from the front door. "Jesse's here!"

"Jesse?" Peter echoed, pushing away from his desk. "What's he doing here?" He was right in the middle of working on his latest scheme for Camp Clearwater, an overnight campout at the lake, but he left his room immediately and trotted for the door, curious.

Peter's mother had let Jesse into the living room, where he had already staked out an armchair. He looked up as Peter walked in, a serious expression on his face.

"I'm here about Jason," he announced, dispensing with greetings. "He's having a hard time lately."

You're telling me? Peter thought, taken aback.

He knew Jesse had a special fondness for young Jason Fairchild, but Jason and Peter went back a lot further. Peter had been worrying about Jason's status as a foster child ever since the boy had joined Junior Explorers—long before Jesse had moved to Missouri. Now that Jason was up for adoption, though, things had become more volatile. Hurt by the fact that his own parents hadn't completed the court-ordered program that would have allowed him to return to one of them and worried that no one else would want him, Jason's typically mischievous behavior had turned darker. Twelve days before, he had been suspended from camp for punching his best friend, Danny, in the mouth. He had returned on Monday, sullen and withdrawn, and had spent the week avoiding talking to Danny or anyone else. Peter had hoped that the other kids would draw Jason out of his shell, but they had ignored him, apparently scared of what else he might do.

Peter was scared too. He was scared for Jason.

"Do you want me to switch him back into my group?" he asked hopefully, dropping onto the couch.

Peter had kept Jason with him at camp at least half the time, until Jason and Jesse had both insisted that Jason be permanently assigned to Jesse's group. Peter's feelings had been secretly hurt, but he had given Jason his way, figuring it was a small enough thing to do if it made him happy.

"No," Jesse said quickly. "I just want to know what else I can do. To help Jason out, I mean."

"Not much. Unless your parents want to adopt him." Peter hadn't meant to be brusque, but the question annoyed him. Did Jesse honestly believe that if he knew a way to help Jason, he wouldn't have already done it?

Jesse rolled his eyes. "I said I wanted to *help* the kid, not put him in therapy for life. I turned seventeen last week, you know—I'm outta there in a year. You'd better come up with something else."

There *was* nothing else, though, and they both knew it. Jason's problems were too big for a couple of teenagers to solve. Even the adults in Jason's life couldn't come up with an answer.

"Just . . . keep being his friend," Peter advised, not sure what else to say. "When he's bad, don't let it faze

23

you. He's only testing, trying to find out who's going to stick by him."

"I know that."

"Maybe try to help him make up with Danny," Peter suggested. "It had to be hard for him, being the Lone Ranger all last week."

Jesse nodded impatiently. "But every time I tried to get him to play with someone else, I got attitude on both sides."

"If you want to put him back in my group . . . ," Peter offered again.

"I can deal with this Danny thing," Jesse said quickly. "Everyone just needed some time to cool off. I'll get it all smoothed over next week."

"Well, that will help. For now," Peter said. "As far as the rest of it goes, we'll just have to wait and see."

Jesse left soon after, saying something about having to go cut his grass, and Peter returned to the project on his desk—permission slips for the overnight to send home with the kids the following week. Since Camp Clearwater was a day camp, the campers never had a chance to sleep out under the stars, a situation Peter intended to remedy. They'd build a campfire, sing songs, make s'mores, play flashlight hide-and-seek, and do all those fun summertime things. All he needed was for a couple of parents to act as chaperones and for everyone to bring a few groceries to share. . . .

Except that now that Jesse had him thinking

about Jason, Peter couldn't concentrate on divvying up donuts and Hi-C anymore. Was it possible there was some way of helping the boy that he had overlooked?

Maybe Jesse and I could do more. Like help Jason's social worker talk him up to potential adoptive families.

Peter suspected that someone, somewhere had a file on all the trouble Jason had gotten into during his time as a foster child, and he was afraid that file was all people would look at.

Or maybe we could even help them out with finding a home for Jason. Peter tried to think of families he knew with children about Jason's age. A family that already had little kids might barely notice one more. There had to be someone at church, or at school . . . somewhere in Clearwater Crossing.

I'll keep an eye out, Peter decided. *The right family's out there, and I'd love to find it.*

"Min! *No!*" Melanie cried, running to stop her fluffy white kitten from climbing farther up the draperies framing the Andrewses' library windows. The cat's needle-sharp claws curled through the fabric, snagging threads as Melanie extracted them one by one.

"What are you doing in here?" she scolded. "Do you know how bad this is?"

Melanie was glad her father had decided to go in to work at his new job for a few hours that afternoon and wasn't around to see Min's latest misbehavior. When she'd brought the kitten home from Aunt Gwen's, Melanie had promised to keep it under control, but so far that wasn't working too well. One corner of her bedspread had turned into a scratching post, the kitten missed the litter box in Melanie's bathroom at least half the time, and every time the bedroom door opened a crack, the little devil bolted, eager to explore the big world outside.

"You're so naughty," Melanie said fondly, nuzzling the kitten against her face as she carried it back to her room. "Who made you so naughty?"

The kitten started to purr, blissfully unaware it was in trouble. Melanie tucked it between the pillows at the head of her unmade bed, then slipped back out the door and quickly shut it behind her. She had slept late and skipped breakfast, and now her stomach was growling, driving her down to the kitchen.

I wish Jesse wasn't tied up with yard work today, she thought, walking barefoot down the cool marble of her stairway. She and Jesse saw each other every day at camp, but they were usually far too busy being counselors to do more than say hello. It wasn't until late in the afternoon, when the Junior Explorers' bus pulled out of the lake parking lot on its way back into town, that her quality time with Jesse began.

They went out nearly every night now, taking full advantage of summertime's slow schedule. The previous Wednesday they had celebrated Jesse's seventeenth birthday at Le Papillon, just the two of them. Melanie had given him a vintage Hawaiian shirt and a watercolor she'd done of the clearing up at camp. He'd given her a book of poems, ignoring her protests that it was *his* birthday. The whole evening had been better than perfect—filet mignon and candlelight and slow, slow dancing . . .

Melanie smiled as she strolled into the kitchen, knowing she'd see him that night and probably talk to him twice more before then. Maybe they'd go to a movie or, better still, rent a couple of videos and watch them in her poolhouse. Later they might go cruising in Jesse's BMW, the windows open to let the warm night air rush over them, or perhaps they'd take a moonlit walk in the fields behind her house, their heads surrounded by drifts of fireflies. There were plenty of possibilities, and Melanie turned each one over in her mind, savoring all it had to offer, as she walked past the breakfast bar.

"What's that?"

An envelope had been propped between salt and pepper shakers at the near end of the counter, where Melanie was sure to see it. Her name sprawled in blue marker across the pink paper, her father's handwriting unmistakable. Melanie popped the seal curiously, smiling at the photograph of a white kitten on the glossy card inside. The only words were those her father had written himself:

Dear Mel,
*Remember when we talked about private art lessons? I
hired a teacher for you who's supposed to be a whiz with
oils. He'll be here at 2:00 today. Enjoy!*

Love,
Dad

"Today?" Melanie exclaimed, checking the clock
built into the oven. Two o'clock wasn't even two
hours away!

Grabbing some Pop-Tarts from the cupboard, not
daring to waste the time it would take to toast them,
she turned and ran back up the stairs. She was still
wearing her shorty pajamas and had yet to take a
shower, but that wasn't her biggest problem.

Where are we going to paint?

Surely her father didn't want them using Mrs. Andrews's studio? Ever since Melanie's mother had
died, the studio had become the closest thing to a
shrine in her atheist father's life.

And what are we going to paint with?

There were lots of supplies in the studio, and
Melanie raided them often, but they were all old,
many of the tubes of paint half dried out. A professional artist was going to expect a little more to
work with.

*Maybe I can organize the good stuff into something
approaching a set,* she thought, pulling open the studio door and skidding into the sunlit room. There

28

were no blinds on the floor-to-ceiling windows in the studio and the summer sun spilled through them, illuminating the bright red bow on top of a box that definitely hadn't been there the last time Melanie had painted. Walking forward, she lifted the box's beribboned lid and smiled down at its contents—a brand-new assortment of oil paints and brushes. New canvases were propped up on the easels. Her father had thought of everything.

Everything except warning me, she thought, running for her bathroom. A total stranger was coming over and she hadn't even washed her hair!

Three

"Wow!" Jenna breathed, awed by her first glimpse of the interior of Beautiful Brides. All the Conrad women had driven to Mapleton that Monday morning to help Caitlin pick out her wedding dress, but now Jenna blocked the doorway, taking in the scenery.

Wedding dresses were everywhere, hung on high chrome racks along the walls and adorning mannequins on carpeted pedestals throughout the room. Jenna saw sequins, beads, embroidery, feathers, even delicate white fur decorating fabrics that ranged from chiffon to velvet. Most of the dresses were white, their full skirts spilling off the pedestals and making milky pools on the sea-green carpet. There were ivory gowns as well, though, and a few in the palest, most pastel shades of pink, blue, and green. Brighter dresses in the back were for bridesmaids, and Jenna's heart skipped with anticipation. All of the sisters were going to be bridesmaids, and Jenna could barely wait to see what she'd be wearing.

"Will you move already?" Mary Beth, the oldest, said impatiently behind her. "You make a better door than window."

"She makes a *lousy* door, if you want the kind that opens," Maggie sniggered, full of her fourteen-year-old self. She had always been annoying, but now that she was getting ready to start high school, she'd become practically unbearable, hanging out with a new group of friends who did nothing but gossip, giggle, and make themselves over at least twice a day.

Jenna ignored her, turning to Caitlin instead as everyone walked inside.

"How will you ever choose?" she asked, eyeing the glass cases in the center of the room, where veils, tiaras, and hair ornaments glittered among the largest selection of gloves Jenna had ever seen. There were satin ones, and lace ones, and the kind that came up over the elbow.

"Oh, you have to wear gloves!" Jenna exclaimed. "I always wanted to wear long gloves. That's the best part of the whole outfit."

"I think maybe I'd better pick a dress first," Caitlin said uncertainly.

"I like the lace gloves," said Sarah, limping toward the display cases. She had recently begun using a regular, straight cane, but she had to lean on it heavily. Sometimes it still made Jenna angry that the drunk driver who'd hit Sarah had simply walked away while Sarah was relearning how to walk, but mostly she tried to focus on what a miracle it was to have her youngest sister with them at all.

"And those shoes with all the rhinestones," Sarah added, pointing with her free hand.

Shoes? Jenna hadn't even noticed the shoes, but she saw them now, lining a big, shelved alcove near the bridesmaids' dresses. "Not rhinestones," she said firmly. "But what about those satin ones with the open toes?"

"Are you going to wear white?" Allison asked Caitlin. "You're going to, right? I don't like those colors. Those aren't really wedding dresses."

"White . . . or maybe light gray, like a silver."

"Gray!" Jenna protested. "No way! Mom, tell her she can't wear gray."

"It's Caitlin's wedding," Mrs. Conrad said dryly. "She can wear an orange vinyl miniskirt if she wants to."

All the girls looked at her, aghast.

"Not that I think she will," their mother admitted, laughing.

"She won't find one here, anyway," a smiling saleswoman reassured them, joining the family group. "I'm Barb, and I'd love to help you with whatever you need."

Caitlin stared at the floor, suddenly shy, so Mrs. Conrad took over, introducing Caitlin as the bride and the rest of the girls as bridesmaids. "We need everything," she said. "Outfits for all of them. And do you have any dresses for the mother of the bride?"

"Oh, yes," Barb said eagerly, probably adding up her commission. "We have everything, right down to toasting goblets and engraved cake servers. But perhaps we should start with Caitlin's gown? That's the most important thing, after all. What kind of dress were you thinking of, dear?"

Caitlin managed to rip her eyes off the carpet. "Something simple," she said quietly. "Long, but not too fancy. Maybe in silver-gray?"

"Or white," Jenna and Allison said in unison.

"You should go backless," Mary Beth said, feeling the lace on a nearby mannequin.

Caitlin looked horrified.

"I don't think so," Mrs. Conrad ruled quickly. "Not for a morning wedding."

Barb led them all back to a large white-doored changing room with mirrors on every wall and a bright light overhead. A few sample veils hung from pegs at the top of the mirrors, ready to be tried on. Outside the room were enough chairs for everyone to wait in. Barb asked for Caitlin's size, then disappeared to retrieve some possible choices.

"What? We're just supposed to sit here while a saleswoman picks things out?" Jenna said. "Why don't we go look through the dresses ourselves?"

"Go ahead," said Mary Beth, lolling back in a chair. "No one's stopping you."

33

"I will," Jenna retorted, starting to head back to the floor. As she did, though, she spotted Barb coming back with a rolling rack of dresses and realized she might miss something. "After this," she added.

"I only have one silver dress, and I don't know if you'll like it," Barb told Caitlin, parking her rack outside the dressing room. "It's very pretty, but it's not exactly simple."

She held the dress up for Caitlin's inspection: a tight, sleeveless sheath of silver satin, bugle-beaded all over, with a long slit up the narrow back. Jenna grudgingly had to admit that gray looked a whole lot better than she had envisioned, but she still didn't want Cat to wear it.

"Would you like to try it on?" Barb asked.

Jenna held her breath, letting it out with relief when Caitlin shook her head.

"It's a little . . . *more* than I was looking for," Caitlin said.

Barb nodded sympathetically. "More of a nighttime dress," she said, returning it to the rack. "And— I'll be honest with you—more of a dress for a second wedding. As young as you are, I'm assuming this is your first?"

Caitlin blushed furiously.

"Of course," Mrs. Conrad said quickly.

"This one is very pretty," Barb said, pulling a traditional white satin dress from the rack. The low-cut

34

bodice was covered with glossy white lace, and satin buttons nestled in matching loops all the way down the back. A long train spilled out behind, edged in the same lace as the bodice.

"Oh, Caitlin!" Sarah exclaimed. "You'll look like a princess in that one!"

Jenna couldn't say anything, temporarily struck dumb by such perfection.

"I don't think I want a train," Caitlin said.

"No train?" Jenna blurted out, shocked. "How can you not want a train? The train is the best part!"

"I thought long gloves were the best part," Mary Beth reminded her snidely.

Barb put the dress back on the rack and pulled out an ivory one. "This candlelight is a flattering color. And you'll see there's a bit of a train, but it's more like the skirt is just longer in back. It barely drags behind you."

"No, white is better!" Jenna said. "Try on that first one, Caitlin."

"If she doesn't like it . . . ," Mrs. Conrad began.

"Can I see that one?" Caitlin asked, pointing to a plain-looking thing near the end.

Barb pulled out a satin dress with an overskirt of chiffon. The neckline was scooped, but not too low. The above-the-elbow sleeves were of puffed chiffon, and the bodice gathered beneath the bust-line, peasant-style, before the skirt fell straight to the floor. The color was rich vanilla white.

"That's pretty, Caitlin," Mrs. Conrad offered. "Do you like that one?"

"Yes. I'll try that on," Caitlin said.

"It's awfully plain," Jenna objected, looking longingly at all the lace and sequins still on the rack. "It's barely even a wedding dress."

Jenna's mother gave her a significant look, her auburn eyebrows raised in silent warning.

"But I suppose when you put on the veil . . . ," she added quickly. "Maybe attached to one of those diamond tiaras. That would be really pretty."

Caitlin frowned. "I was thinking of wearing a hat."

"A hat!" Jenna gasped. "No, Caitlin! It *has* to be a veil."

Dodging into the dressing room, she grabbed one off a hook and put it on her own head. "See how pretty?" she insisted, ignoring the fact that she was also wearing a tank top.

"This dress would look pretty with either," Barb said diplomatically. "Why don't you try it on while I go get some hats and maybe a few veils?"

Jenna gave the woman a grateful look.

"And while you're doing that, maybe I can get your sisters started trying on some bridesmaids' dresses for size," Barb added, earning a second grateful look, this one from Mrs. Conrad. "Did you have a color in mind for the bridesmaids?"

Caitlin hesitated.

36

"Royal blue," Jenna said happily. "They're going to be blue. Right, Cat?"

"Well, that was before," her sister said softly. "When I thought my dress would be silver. But if I'm going to wear white . . . maybe yellow?" She looked questioningly at her mother.

Mrs. Conrad nodded. "Whatever you want."

"Yellow is very pretty for a morning wedding," Barb said encouragingly.

"*Yellow?*" Jenna wailed, unable to contain herself any longer. "No one looks good in yellow!"

Caitlin stared at her, stricken. Mrs. Conrad's foot nudged Jenna's knee.

"Let your sister make her own decisions," she said.

"I mean, uh, there are probably lots of colors, and Caitlin probably wants to see them all," Jenna said, covering. "Right, Cat?"

"Sure. Okay." Caitlin smiled weakly before retreating into the dressing room with the white chiffon and closing the door behind her.

"Smooth," Mary Beth muttered, jabbing Jenna with an elbow, but Jenna ignored her. Yellow dresses were a disaster they'd *all* thank her for averting.

"I'm going to go get a tiara for Cat to try on," she announced, sailing out of the dressing area. "And some of those long gloves."

The way things were going so far, Caitlin obviously needed all the advice Jenna could give her!

*   *   *

37

"I don't know what's wrong with me!" Leah exclaimed, scratching the fronts of both thighs at once. The skin between her knees and shorts was pink and strangely bumpy, long red streaks attesting to the number of passes her fingernails had already made. "Do you think it's poison ivy?"

Miguel shrugged. "Looks like it. It doesn't look good, that's for sure."

The two of them were standing by themselves on the lakeshore while the campers swam that Monday afternoon. From their position beneath a shady tree, Leah could just make out Peter's brother on the end of the short dock, a curving stretch of green water in front of him. Jesse, Melanie, Ben, and Peter stood evenly spaced along the sand, completing that day's lifeguard squad. Nicole and Jenna were both absent, having taken the day off.

"It's spread around the back now too," Leah said, twisting her body to see. The patches of skin behind her knees were especially nasty-looking, a few of the bumps having grown into small, oozing blisters. "I can't believe this! Why now?"

She had managed to go all summer without getting poison ivy, and suddenly she had the worst case any of them had ever seen.

"I mean, I thought *maybe* those bushes might be poison ivy when I went in to get the softball," she admitted, "but I never got it *before*. I sure never got it like this!"

38

"All my guys have had it off and on since practically the first day of camp. Although I have to say that yours is a particularly lovely case." Miguel smiled. "We ought to call this place Camp Calamine."

Leah was not amused.

"But Miguel," she whined, "I don't want to be red and itchy tonight. I thought you were coming over!"

Her parents had been gone two whole days already, and Miguel still hadn't been by the condo. He knew they were gone. She knew he knew they were gone. But to Leah's surprise, her boyfriend hadn't been quick to suggest they make use of all that privacy. In fact, he hadn't suggested it at all. She honestly didn't know whether to be insulted or relieved; it had certainly never occurred to her that *she* might have to be the one to press the issue.

"It looks like the only thing you're going to be doing tonight is taking a nice long oatmeal bath," Miguel said. "And you don't need me there for that."

"Maybe I do," Leah said, trying for a seductive look.

"Yeah. Pass." He laughed. "That stuff is contagious, you know. There's some kind of oil involved. You'd better stop scratching, too, or you're going to spread it all over yourself."

"It's killing me!" Leah said through gritted teeth. "You have no idea how this itches."

"Peter has a bottle of calamine up in the cabin.

Why don't you go use it before you do more damage?"

"That's going to look so awful," she groaned, imagining the chalky pink lotion against her dark tan.

"Don't take this the wrong way, okay? But it already looks pretty awful. You might as well be comfortable."

"Yeah, all right. I'll be back in a few minutes."

She set out for the cabin in the clearing at the center of camp, turning around again when she heard Miguel dive into the lake behind her.

"Who wants to race me?" he challenged the kids, splashing water in all directions.

"I do! I do!" a dozen voices yelled.

Leah smiled as she watched the campers attack her boyfriend, pushing, laughing, and trying to climb up his bare back.

He's such a good guy, she thought. *I'm so lucky to have him.*

She watched a moment longer, wondering if she should insist on his coming over that night anyway. She hadn't expected to be the one who made the first move, but the fact that he wasn't pushing was making her feel strangely bolder. After all, they were ready for this. Right?

The persistent itching behind her knees wheeled her around and sent her scurrying for the cabin.

There'll be plenty of time later, she decided as she

ran. *Not to mention that things will be a lot more romantic when I'm not covered in calamine lotion!*

"Oh, good, Benny. You're back," said Mrs. Pipkin, looking up from the magazine she was reading. "I need my car keys."

"Now?" Ben had just stepped in through the garage door, hot and sweaty from a long day at camp, and his plans had involved showering quickly and then driving by Bernie's.

Mrs. Pipkin checked the watch on her thick wrist. "Well, in about fifteen minutes anyway. I joined that new weight-loss clinic in town, and my first appointment's this evening. Isn't that exciting?"

Exciting? Ben was floored! His mother had never dieted before. He tried to imagine her at a normal size—not thin, just not head-turningly large—and found he couldn't even do it.

"Say something," she prompted. "Dr. Fowler said it would be better for me if I lost some weight."

"*Way* better," Ben agreed, finding his voice again. "We studied that in school."

As overweight as his mother was, she was a setup for diabetes, heart problems, and a bunch of other bad things. Not to mention how she looked. The thought of her actually losing weight was terrific . . . amazing . . . almost too good to be true.

Now, if I could just get Dad *a makeover . . .*

41

Mrs. Pipkin hefted herself up out of the dining room chair. She was wearing a new flowered caftan that billowed, tentlike, to her round calves. Her bell-shaped sleeve fell away from her arm as she held out her hand, palm up. "Keys?"

"How about . . . how about I drive you?" Ben offered, his excitement tempered by his burning desire to keep control of the car. He hadn't seen Bernie since Saturday afternoon, and he was going through withdrawal. "I could drop you off and pick you up when you're done."

"I'm only going to be there an hour."

"An hour?" Ben managed to stifle his groan. "All right. So I'll pick you up in an hour, then. Come on, Mom, I need to drive by a friend's house."

"You *need* to," she teased, the corners of her smile disappearing into fleshy cheeks. "Well, you're not driving me like that. Any chauffeur of mine is going to smell a whole lot better than you do."

"Five minutes!" Ben promised, racing for the shower.

Ten minutes later they were in the car, Mrs. Pipkin calling out every turn as they drove toward the weight-loss clinic.

"It's right up there at the corner of Chestnut and Main," she said for the third time. "They took over the old luggage store."

"All right." Ben's mind was only half on his driving as he tried to map out the shortest route from downtown to Bernie's house in his head.

"Right there!" his mother said, pointing ahead to the other side of the street. "Do you see it, Benny?"

"I see it, I see it," Ben muttered, hitting the turn signal. There were a couple of people standing on the sidewalk in front of the former luggage store, the windows of which were plastered with posters announcing the grand opening of Slenderific Studios. Ben was just beginning a U-turn to park at the open stretch of curb in front when the door suddenly opened and the last person in the world he would have expected to see at a weight-loss studio walked out, all skinny legs and angles and short light brown hair.

Bernie!

His brain nearly melted at the thought of running into her. There. With his mother. His hands froze on the steering wheel and his right foot kicked reflexively, pressing the gas pedal toward the floor.

"Benny! Benny, what are you doing?" his mother protested. "You're passing it!"

"Parking . . . in back," he panted, his heart thundering in his chest. "I think . . . there's parking . . . off the alley."

"There was parking right in front!"

"Was there? Oh, well." Ben whipped the car around two corners, cruising back up the alley behind the

43

clinic. Luckily, there was a parking lot, which he pulled into too fast, stopping cockeyed across two spaces.

"Okay! Here we are," he said, jumping out to pull her door open.

"What is the *matter* with you?" she demanded, easing herself onto the pavement.

"Better hurry or you're going to be late. I'll catch you in an hour." He was driving away before she could protest, retracing his route to where he had just seen Bernie.

"Bernie! Bernie!" he called urgently, pulling up to the curb. She was walking along the sidewalk, but hadn't gone far.

"Ben!" she exclaimed, stepping over to the car. "What are you doing here?"

"Get in," he said tensely, praying she'd do it before his mother looked out the clinic windows.

"But—"

"Hurry!"

Bernie climbed in on the passenger side, her brown eyes wide. "What's going on?" she asked as he drove off down the street.

Ben took a deep breath, trying to slow both his heart rate and his driving now that he was out of his mother's sight. "Nothing?"

"But what are you doing here?"

"I was just bringing—" He cut himself off abruptly, realizing that he should have thought of a good cover story before he picked her up. "What are *you* doing here?" he countered. "What do you need with a weight-loss clinic?"

"With a weight-loss clinic?" Suddenly Bernie seemed like the nervous one. She chewed her raspberry-glossed bottom lip, so cute Ben's heart flipped over. "How did you see me come out of the clinic? I thought you just pulled up."

Back to me, Ben thought, afraid he was losing their verbal tennis match.

"Well . . . I, uh . . . I *saw* you when I was driving the other way," he said. "And then I had to go down the street and turn around. And there were . . . uh, stop signs."

Bernie dropped her eyes to her bare knees. She usually favored loose gauzy dresses or cutoff jeans, but that afternoon she was wearing crisp white shorts and a button-down shirt. "I kind of got a job there," she admitted. "I started today."

"A job? Doing what?"

"Well . . . I'm kind of . . . setting up their computers."

Ben was so shocked he had to pull over and stop the car. Bernie was only fourteen, and some business had hired her to work on their computers?

"It's nothing!" she said quickly. "Just a little network and a database of their clients. Anyone could do it. And since my mom knows Mrs. Winston, the owner . . ." Bernie shrugged. "It's mostly data entry."

"But they're paying you?"

"Well . . . yeah."

Ben shook his head, impressed. He had known Bernie was interested in computers, but she had always insisted she didn't know that much about them. He felt stupid now to think how he had bragged about his own programming ability.

Then another thought struck him, and all he felt was fear.

"You're doing data entry?" he repeated.

"Yeah. Mostly. I enter all the stuff about their new clients. Name, address, how much they weigh . . . that type of thing."

Oh, no, Ben thought. *No, this can't be happening.*

If Bernie was working there, entering data, sooner or later she'd run into his *mother's* data. Worse, sooner or later, she'd run into his mother!

No way. I definitely can't let that happen.

But how was he going to stop it?

Four

"Not again," Nicole whispered, tears pooling in her lower lashes. She had finally managed to lose a pound, and now she had gained it again. "I shouldn't have gone to that matinee with Courtney and Gail yesterday!"

All they had done was sit in the dark for hours and eat so much candy Nicole had lost track. The shows hadn't even been good—a double feature of those stupid horror movies Courtney loved. Nicole could barely imagine the new-age Courtney she'd been putting up with since the prom enjoying anything as unenlightening as horror, but the old Courtney was back now. With a vengeance.

"I hear that if you eat Red Vines and M&M's in combination, the calories cancel each other out," she'd said, with a glance at Gail to make sure her new friend wasn't missing such sterling wit. Nicole, of course, had a box of each of those candies.

"I've heard that too," Gail said. "And if you wash them down with soda, they practically just burn up on impact."

"This is *diet* soda," Nicole had said defensively, sending them both into fits of laughter.

"That's okay, then," Gail had said, still laughing. "It's all about the soda."

Now Nicole stepped tearfully off the scale, wondering what she'd been thinking. If she'd just gone to camp, like she was supposed to, she could have kept that pound off and maybe even lost another. It wasn't as if she'd *enjoyed* being the butt of Courtney and Gail's mean jokes. And the dumbest part was that she knew they didn't even think she was fat—they were just doing it to bug her.

It definitely bugged her.

Well, that's what you get, she told herself, the tears finally spilling over as she walked back into her bedroom. *You think if you lose weight one day, you can eat whatever you want the next? You are such a pig!*

Glancing at the clock on her desk, she saw that if she didn't hurry up, she was going to miss camp again that Tuesday. Neither of her parents had been willing to lend her a car that morning, which meant she'd have to ride her bike to Clearwater Crossing Park and catch the bus to camp along with the kids. Wiping her tears away impatiently, still angry with herself, Nicole dug through her dresser and pulled out her ugliest, sloppiest T-shirt and a pair of faded drawstring shorts, ignoring other, much cuter clothes that still fit her perfectly well.

You deserve to be punished, she told herself harshly. *A pig like you doesn't deserve to wear anything cute.*

She shoved her bare feet into sneakers and ran down the stairs to the kitchen.

I should have grapefruit for breakfast. And salad for lunch. I could take it in a Ziploc and then throw the bag away.

But eating grapefruit and chopping up salad took time, and as soon as Nicole saw her mother and Heather sitting at the kitchen table, she knew that produce would have to wait. All she wanted was to grab something and leave before anyone could start talking to her about the baby again.

"There you are, Nicole," Mrs. Brewster greeted her cheerfully. "Do you want a waffle? There's some batter left."

Nicole's stomach growled at the aroma filling the kitchen, and the syrup on her mother's and younger sister's empty plates looked good enough to lick up. She hesitated, tempted.

"We're picking out baby names," Heather added, holding up a paperback book. "It's really fun."

"No thanks. I'm in a hurry," Nicole said bitterly, turning to the kitchen cupboards instead.

She snapped a lunch sack open, annoyed that she had to rush while her mom just sat there, wasting time, not even using the car. The fact that Nicole would have left the car sitting, unusable, in the lake parking lot all day was something she refused to think about.

"What time are you getting home?" her mother asked.

"Don't know," Nicole answered, dropping food into her bag: a six-pack of Oreo cookies for breakfast, peanut butter–filled crackers for lunch, an individual pack of cheese puffs. There was nothing even resembling health food in the Brewster kitchen that morning, let alone food for people on diets. Her previously slender mother had gone totally off the deep end since she'd gotten pregnant, using the baby as an excuse for eating every kind of junk food. Nicole found some raisins and dropped in a couple of boxes before closing up her bag. Raisins were full of calories too, but at least they had some claim to nutritional value.

"I thought you might like to do some shopping with me and Heather this afternoon," Mrs. Brewster persisted. "For the baby. I want to get that sewing room converted to a nursery before I get too big to do it. Heather and I are going to look for a crib, and maybe a changing table."

"You know what? I'm going to be busy," said Nicole. She'd make sure of it now.

"You're not hanging out with Gail again, are you?" Her mother's voice had lost a little of its lilt, and Nicole couldn't help smiling. Not that long ago, before the Wienerageous disaster, Gail had had all the adults so fooled into believing she was a model teen that Nicole's parents had *wanted* Nicole to hang out with her, hoping some of that virtue might rub off. Now that the real Gail was back on the scene, though, everything had changed; Nicole's parents were terrified of what might rub off now.

"Yep, that's the plan," said Nicole, smiling as if she didn't know what her mother was thinking. "Gotta go now."

She grabbed a couple of juice boxes and hurried out to the garage before her mother could say more.

If I call Courtney from the park, I probably can hook up with her and Gail after camp, Nicole thought, checking her backpack to make sure she had some change. Swinging the straps over her shoulders, she pushed the button for the garage-door opener and rode her bicycle out into a perfect summer morning.

If my being with Gail bothers Mom that much, a few sarcastic comments about my weight are totally worth it!

"Now, make sure you get these signed by your parents," Peter said, passing out permission slips at the Tuesday afternoon assembly.

The campers squirmed excitedly on the long, split-log benches in the center of camp, grabbing eagerly for the papers. Everyone was talking loudly, thrilled about the overnight campout Peter had just announced, and there was more than a little pushing as kids tried to climb their neighbors to get a permission slip faster.

"Take it easy," Peter told them. "The overnight isn't until next Thursday—that's like nine days away—so getting your permission slip a minute later than someone else won't make a bit of difference."

Amy Robbins raised her hand. "I'm going to ask my daddy to come."

"Good. I hope he'll be able to." There was a line on the form for parents to sign up, but Peter wasn't really worried about chaperones anymore. In addition to Eight Prime, Chris Hobart and his girlfriend, Maura, David Altmann, and Mr. Altmann were all coming—anyone else was gravy.

"But the main thing is food," Peter added. "Later this week, Jenna will have the grocery assignments for everyone who's coming, so try to get this paper signed right away, and make sure your parents write down their names if they want to camp out with us. Otherwise, we won't have enough and you kids will have to take turns going hungry," he teased.

"I'm not going hungry!" Jason said, his blue eyes round with outrage. It was the first thing Peter had heard him say for days.

Jesse was sitting next to Jason. "He was kidding, bud," he said quickly.

A few of the other kids started laughing. Jason glared at them.

"Okay! Let's take a look at these permission slips," Peter said, anxious to smooth things over. He waved one above his head to get their attention again. "See that list at the top? That's the stuff you'll need to bring."

He read off the items as the campers followed along, chatting excitedly. Most of the things were routine: a change of clothes, shoes, a bathing suit, a hat, sunscreen, bug repellent. But when he got to the bottom of the list—two large sports bottles of water, a flashlight with fresh batteries, and a sleeping bag with a pillow—the kids really started getting excited.

"I have a Barbie sleeping bag," Lisa announced proudly. "It's pink."

"You might want to bring a tarp to put under it, then," Jenna told her. "Pink's not going to hold up too well in the dirt."

"We're sleeping in the dirt?" said Priscilla. "Cool!"

"Not *in* the dirt, *on* the dirt," Jenna amended quickly. "Or on the grass, if we can find some."

"I have a tent," said Danny. "I'm going to bring it."

"Me too!" said a couple more voices.

"I don't have one," somebody wailed.

Peter had been afraid of that, which was why he had left tents off the list in the first place. They weren't necessary.

"It will be more fun if nobody brings a tent," he said, for the sake of those without them. "We're all going to be sleeping around the campfire together and we want to be able to talk and tell stories. Besides, when you sleep in a tent, you can't see the stars."

"I'm bringing mine," Danny said stubbornly.

Peter sighed. Maybe he could talk to Danny's folks.

"So, are we ready to go home?" David asked, walking up behind Peter. "I've got places to go and people to see." He winked, and Peter knew his brother meant Caitlin.

"Everybody, put your permission slips in your backpacks and walk with your group to the bus," Peter shouted. "Let's get moving! Your driver's in a hurry."

Papers were stuffed into packs, and counselors surged to their feet in an effort to control the stampede that followed. The kids were still charged up about the overnight—which was the main reason Peter had waited until the end of the day to announce it—and there was plenty of shouting and pushing as they poured off of the benches and streamed across the clearing toward the trail to the parking lot. The counselors were swept along with them, giving up on dividing the tide into organized groups and simply riding the wave.

We'll just have to count them again at the bus to make sure everyone gets there, Peter thought, preparing to bring up the rear as a further precaution. The clearing had already emptied and only a few stragglers were still visible at the trailhead. To Peter's surprise, Jason Fairchild was the last in line, his white-blond hair making him easy to spot.

"Hey, Jason," Peter greeted him, catching up. "What happened to the rest of your group?"

Jason shrugged. Peter couldn't even see Jesse up ahead; he and nearly everyone else had disappeared into the trees.

"You'd better put that permission slip in your bag before you lose it," he advised, matching his pace to the boy's. Jason took a few more slow steps, then stopped and crumpled the paper in his hand, dropping the wad on the trail.

"I'm not going anyway," he said sullenly.

"What! Why not?"

"It's going to be stupid."

"It's going to be fun!"

Jason's gaze was on his sneakers, their laces frayed and full of knots. "I don't want to go."

Kneeling down, Peter took the boy by the shoulders. Jason lifted his baby-blue eyes, a shock of soft color in a pale, freckled face.

"*Why* don't you want to go?" Peter asked.

Jason tried and failed to squirm out of Peter's grip. "I . . . I don't have a sleeping bag."

"Is that all?" Peter exclaimed. "You're not going to be the only one in that boat, Jason. It's right there on the permission slip for people to mark whether they

55

need a sleeping bag or can lend one. We probably have five of them at my house. I'll lend you one of ours."

Jason shook his head. "I want my *own!*" he said petulantly.

"For Pete's sake, Jason, stop whining. You can't always get what you want."

Peter could have bitten his tongue out when he saw the hurt look Jason gave him and realized who he'd just said that to. "I mean, things like sleeping bags just don't matter," he added quickly. "I know it seems like they do when you're little, but you have to trust me, Jason. This is nothing."

Jason sniffed loudly and wiped at the tears that had started to fall. "I don't want to go. Everyone's stupid parents are coming to watch us. What are we? A bunch of babies?"

So that's the problem. Jason's afraid he'll be the only one on the overnight without a parent. Peter's heart ached for the little boy whose childhood had been so different from his own.

"Listen, Jason," he reassured him. "Everyone's parents are *not* going to be there. It's going to be mostly kids, I promise—and it won't be fun without you. Besides, I was thinking you might be able to help me out with something important."

Jason sniffed again, but he looked a little more hopeful. "What?"

"Well, I can't tell you what it is right now, but if you come, I'll give you a special job," Peter promised, figuring he ought to be able to think of one before next Thursday.

"I'll have to ask my foster mom," Jason said uncertainly. "Maybe she won't let me go."

"*I'll* ask Mrs. Brown." Peter picked the permission slip up off the ground and motioned for Jason to start walking.

"When I went to winter camp, she had to ask my social worker."

"Then I'll ask your social worker, too," Peter said, shepherding Jason up the trail.

Actually, there were a few things Peter had been wanting to ask Jason's social worker anyway—like exactly what she was doing in terms of finding Jason a permanent home. Peter had never met the woman, but lately he'd been dying to, if only to impress upon her what a moody, nervous wreck all the adoption stress was making of Jason.

So I'll get her number from Mrs. Brown and I'll call her, he decided. *This overnight gives me the perfect excuse.*

"*Now and always,*" Jenna sang, strumming along on her guitar Tuesday night. "*Love is patient, love is kind. It always protects, always trusts, always perseveres. . . .*"

She stopped and peered down at the music Guy

57

had scribbled out for the new song they'd written for Caitlin's wedding—with a little help from the apostle Paul.

"I don't like that chord," she muttered, squinting at Guy's chicken scratches. She played it again, just to make sure she wasn't hitting a clinker. Her guitar playing had never been great, but if she wanted her new song to be perfect, she was going to have to work out the rough spots herself.

She tried singing the phrase a few different ways, with different chords beneath it, becoming increasingly annoyed when she couldn't improve on what Guy had already written. He and the rest of the band had insisted that the song was just fine, but to Jenna's ears it was still missing something, some little touch to make it special. After all, this was her song, so she ought to get what she wanted. When those guys wrote their own songs, then they could settle.

Maybe Mom could help me out, she thought.

Mrs. Conrad was an excellent piano player. The problem was that to ask for help Jenna would have to tell her mother what she was up to, and the song was supposed to be a surprise. Outside of the band, the only person who knew about it was Peter, and even he didn't know exactly what she was writing. Jenna couldn't wait to see everyone's faces when she unveiled her masterpiece at Caitlin's wedding.

"If it's done by then," she sighed, dropping her guitar onto her bed in frustration. It just cleared her crossed legs, landing in the pile of wedding cake clippings she'd been organizing before she'd realized she ought to work on her song while Caitlin was still out with David. Beneath the clippings, a half-filled sheet in her steno pad represented an abandoned attempt at a grocery list for Camp Clearwater's overnight. "There's just too much to do! How will I ever keep track of it all?"

The grocery list would have to wait, she decided, pulling the pad out from under her guitar and putting it on the ledge behind her bed. Peter wanted the grocery assignments by Friday, but she didn't even know how many people were coming yet. Next she slid the guitar under her bed. Since she couldn't figure out how to fix her song, she might as well give it a rest.

"That leaves cake," she told herself, gathering up the clippings, then spreading them out neatly on her comforter.

Her frustration gradually evaporated as she gazed at the various choices a bride could make in pastry—*if* she planned ahead and found the right baker. Caitlin had actually said something about having their mother make the cake, but that was clearly ridiculous. Mrs. Conrad's cakes were delicious, but how a wedding cake tasted wasn't nearly as important as how it looked.

And it had to look perfect.

Jenna's definite preference was traditional—white,

and the taller the better. But what should be on top? Her clippings showed fresh flowers, porcelain figurines, even bride and groom paper dolls made from photographs of the happy couple. It was nearly impossible to choose, especially since Caitlin hadn't picked her flowers yet.

I'm guessing they're going to be yellow, though.

Despite Jenna's best attempts to steer Caitlin to other colors, a light, buttery yellow had ultimately been selected for the bridesmaids' dresses. Jenna had been disappointed, but at least that shade wasn't as unflattering as the canary she had feared, and she had to admit it seemed right with the wedding dress Caitlin had finally chosen—a simple white lace bodice with a scooped neck and fitted elbow sleeves over a full white skirt.

I'll start on my flower clippings next, Jenna decided. *Just because our dresses are yellow doesn't mean Cat has to limit herself to yellow flowers. And when I know what color the flowers are, then I'll know if I want them on the cake or not.*

Jenna ran through some possibilities in her mind. Bright pink roses would be gorgeous with yellow, and would stand out on a white cake, too. Blue was another way to go. She could just picture the dark blues of iris and delphinium against butter-yellow satin and fluffy white frosting. And a garland on the table around the cake always looked nice....

"What do you think of my hair?" Maggie asked loudly, nearly giving Jenna a heart attack. She'd been so engrossed in planning that she hadn't even heard her younger sister come up the stairs.

"Maggie!" she complained. "You could knock, you know."

"Your door wasn't shut." Maggie came farther into the room and pirouetted in her stocking feet. "They're called finger waves," she announced, pointing to the auburn zigzags plastered to her scalp. The rest of her long curly hair had been wound into a tight knot at the nape of her neck. "I'm thinking of wearing my hair this way for Caitlin's wedding."

"Whoopee," Jenna replied, annoyed by the intrusion. "No one's going to be looking at you anyway."

Maggie bristled. "Yeah? Well, I'm going to ask Caitlin what *she* thinks. *And* I'm going to ask her if we can wear flowered wreaths on our heads."

"No, we can't, because we're going to be carrying bouquets."

Jenna hadn't actually discussed bouquets with Caitlin yet, but she was positive she was right. All the times she had pictured herself walking down the aisle in her bridesmaid dress, she had always been carrying a bouquet.

"I'm going to ask her anyway," Maggie insisted. "I want to wear a wreath."

"Will you stop being such a prima donna? Caitlin's the one who's getting married, not you."

"I—I'm going to ask Mom, then!" Maggie sputtered, turning on her heel and storming out of the room."

"Good! Ask Mom!" Jenna shouted after her. "She'll just tell you the same thing."

Poor Caitlin, Jenna thought, as Maggie disappeared. *I hope I'm not living at home when I start planning my wedding. Having to work around busybodies like Maggie would drive me totally crazy!*

Five

"Why aren't you eating?" Mrs. Pipkin asked Ben at breakfast Wednesday morning. "Don't you feel well?"

"I feel fine," Ben lied, figuring she wasn't inquiring into his mental health anyway. Ever since he'd run into Bernie at Slenderific Studios, his every waking thought had turned upon the horror of her discovery of his nerdly secrets and the inevitable resulting breakup.

"You'd better eat up and get moving, then, if you want your father to drop you off at the bus on his way to work."

"I can't finish all this. You gave me too much."

That part, at least, was true. His mother's plate held only a scoop of cottage cheese, a slice of dry toast, and some grapes, but she seemed to have cooked the usual number of pancakes, dividing them between two plates instead of three.

"I don't know how to mix batter for two yet," she admitted, staring longingly at the butter- and syrup-drenched mess on Ben's plate. "But I guess I'll learn, because it's going to be a long, long time before I taste pancakes again."

"They don't let you have any at all?" Mr. Pipkin asked, finally lifting his eyes from the morning paper. "That seems pretty harsh."

"Yes!" Ben exclaimed, seizing the opportunity that had just presented itself. "What kind of cruel clinic is this? They can't just go around starving people."

If he could talk his mother into quitting her program . . .

"That's what happens when you're fat," she said sadly.

"You're not *that* fat," Ben told her, crossing his fingers under the table.

"I think you're perfect," Mr. Pipkin said, winking at his wife. "As far as I'm concerned, you don't need to change a thing."

"Oh, honey! That's so sweet." She gazed at Ben's father the way she'd been staring at Ben's pancakes just moments before.

"*Or,*" Ben said, thinking quickly. "*Or,* you could just lose the weight on your own and save all that money you'd be spending at the clinic." As much as he didn't want his mother blowing his cover with Bernie, he didn't want to discourage her from losing weight either.

But Mrs. Pipkin shook her head. "I like the clinic, and it's not that expensive. Besides, if I try to do this on my own, I know I won't." She looked down at her bulging ruffled bathrobe. "I never have before."

Ben couldn't argue with that. He pushed his plate away, the pancakes he'd already eaten turning to lead in his belly.

It's over, then, he thought. *Unless something major changes, I can kiss Bernie good-bye.*

He rose from the table with a sigh, so depressed he could barely move.

He hadn't even kissed her hello yet.

"So how's the poison ivy now?" Miguel asked Leah after camp. The Junior Explorers' bus had just set out for home, and the two of them were lingering under some shady trees at the edge of the lake parking lot, postponing the moment they'd have to leave in their separate cars. "You haven't mentioned it for at least ten minutes."

"Very funny," she groaned.

She was wearing long pants that Wednesday, both to cover her ugly rash and to make scratching it more difficult. Beneath the lightweight cotton was a layer of calamine lotion so thick she could feel it cracking. "It's driving me a little less crazy now. Maybe I've turned the corner."

Miguel smiled, a flash of white teeth in a deeply tanned face. Leah had found him handsome when she met him, but the way she loved him more every day had only made him cuter, until now she thought he was just about perfect.

"At least the rash stayed on your legs," he said. "The way you were going after it Monday, I thought you'd have bumps all over your body."

"How horrible!" She shuddered at the thought of trying to keep her hands off that much itchy skin. "Someone would have had to tie me down."

He waggled his dark brows. "Sounds interesting."

"I'm surprised to hear *you* say that," she returned, a bit of sulkiness creeping into her tone.

"What's that supposed to mean?"

She shrugged, but her heart had started racing and she could feel the blood rushing up to her cheeks. "What do you think it means?"

Miguel leaned against a pine tree, his brown eyes locked on hers. "I don't know."

"Do I have to draw you a picture? My parents are out of *town*, Miguel."

"And?"

"And you're acting like you don't even care!"

"What do you expect me to do, Leah?"

She was really blushing now, but she forged ahead anyway. "You were the one saying all those things . . . about how you'd be all alone in that big bed at your new house. . . ."

"What? But you didn't think . . . ? Leah, I was kidding!"

She stared at him, stunned. Miguel was the one who had sparked this idea in her head in the first place—or at least fanned it into flames. And now he was saying she'd misunderstood?

"So you don't . . . want to, then?" she said, so embarrassed that the last few words were just little choking sounds in her throat.

Miguel scrunched his eyes shut. "It's not that I don't *want* to. . . ."

"Then what are we waiting for?" Leah blurted out. "We're in love. We're both eighteen. I mean, that's old by a lot of people's standards. And I'm going to be moving away soon. Meanwhile my parents have given us this perfect opportunity—and we're not even taking advantage of it!"

"I doubt they saw it as that type of opportunity," he said dryly.

"No. But they must have realized there was a chance. . . ." Leah shook her head reflexively. It felt wrong bringing her parents into the discussion. They hadn't actually *told* her not to have Miguel spend the night, but the way they'd kept reminding her to keep the door locked, and to call them if she got scared, and especially the way they'd kept saying how much they trusted her had made it pretty clear they assumed she'd be sleeping alone. She would never do anything to hurt them, but she had to grow up sometime. Right? She had to live her own life.

"Your parents trust you. That's all," said Miguel.

"You're not making this sound more attractive," she said guiltily. "I kind of thought you'd be into it."

He took a deep breath and let it out slowly. "I am. I mean I could be. But . . . I just think we ought to wait."

"Wait?" Wasn't the *girl* supposed to say that? "For how long?"

The question seemed to surprise him. "Well, until we're married. Right?"

Married?

They had barely talked about marriage since February, when they'd broken off their short, impulsive engagement. She'd told him then that if she went away to college, she planned to finish, which meant at least four years apart, longer if she went to graduate school and he insisted on staying in Clearwater Crossing. As much as she still wanted to believe they'd end up married someday, it seemed like wishful thinking. It certainly wasn't something she was counting on.

Was he?

"I mean, won't you just feel better knowing we did things right?" he persisted. "And if we're going to be married in the Church . . . well, you know how they feel about premarital sex."

Leah's eyebrows went up. She also knew how

they felt about performing marriages involving non-Catholics. Was Miguel assuming she'd convert now too? What else was he assuming?

"Just to be sure I understand," she said slowly. "You're telling me you want us both to stay virgins until we're twenty-two. Maybe longer."

He recoiled a bit, wincing. "I never said . . . Look, let's just drop this, okay? I don't want to talk about it anymore."

Leah's heart missed a beat as she tried to read between those lines. Was he saying there had already been someone else? Miguel had seen a lot of different girls before he met her, and had been chased by many more. Any one of them . . . maybe *more* than one of them . . . He certainly hadn't cared about his church's opinion in those first angry years after his father's death.

Maybe Leah was the one who'd been assuming.

"Okay. That's . . . fine. I've got stuff to do anyway," she said, turning away to hide her rising tears. "I'll see you tomorrow," she added, hurrying out into the sunshine.

She rushed across the gravel to her convertible before he could call her back, not wanting him to see her cry. Everything was getting so complicated. She was worried about disappointing her parents . . . and now Miguel was worried about upsetting God? Of course she'd known that deeply religious people believed in waiting for marriage, but since when was Miguel so committed?

You ought to be glad he cares about church again, she told herself. *You're the one who kept pushing him in that direction.*

Which seemed ironic now, when she didn't have a clear faith of her own to draw on. Her mother had been raised Christian and her father Jewish, but Leah herself had been raised to believe that morality could and did exist outside the bounds of religion. Some things were just right, and others were wrong. Unfortunately that still left a few tricky areas, things that every good person had to work out for herself.

If only I had more time! There's just so much pressure on us. On me . . .

And now that he'd tried to take it off, she felt it even more.

"That's good, Melanie!" said her new art teacher, Dan Meadows.

Melanie's hour-long painting lessons were supposed to take place on Sunday afternoons, but since they hadn't accomplished much actual painting the first day, Dan had come by for a second, follow-up lesson that Wednesday evening. A graduate student in the fine arts department at CU, Dan had been so taken with the Andrewses' private studio that, after he'd introduced himself and shown her some of his

70

work, he'd spent most of the remaining time rearranging all the easels, equipment, and supplies until everything was perfect. They had barely touched brush to canvas, beginning work on some background techniques, when he'd announced that he had to leave for another lesson.

"I'll make it up to you," he'd promised, wiping large paint-smudged hands down his faded T-shirt. "First lessons are always hectic, but I'll come by on Wednesday night and we'll finish this hour of painting—no charge. Just to get things started right."

And now here he was, as good as his word, his shaggy head bent enthusiastically over a canvas she hadn't thought particularly stellar. He was wearing shorts and leather sandals, his leg hair curling in little brown licks around his tan ankles.

"I like the way you blended from light to dark," he said, pointing. "That's exactly what we're looking for."

He smiled at her and she felt her breath catch involuntarily. The jury was still out on whether Dan would be a good teacher, but anyone could see he was gorgeous. Melanie had spent most of Sunday telling herself that his total adorableness was *not* the reason she didn't mind him moving all her mom's stuff around the studio, but she hadn't been able to think of a better one.

And she'd been thinking a lot.

71

He's not interested in me, she told herself firmly, ripping her eyes away from his and refocusing them on her brushwork. *And I'm* definitely *not interested in him.*

Even if she wasn't Dan's student, and probably ten years his junior, there was still the not-so-small matter of Jesse. After everything she and Jesse had gone through to finally get together, there was no way she'd do anything that might jeopardize their relationship. Even if the cute way Dan's brown hair curled behind his ears did make her heart beat faster . . .

"Okay," he said, watching her work. "But you want to feather that out. Don't be afraid to let the brush get dry. Can I help you?"

"Sure."

The next thing she knew, Dan was standing against her back, his hand warm on hers as he guided her brush through the strokes. His Wrigley's spearmint breath ruffled her hair. She could feel his chest rise and fall against her shoulders. She stiffened, freaked out both by the contact and the realization that it wasn't entirely unwelcome.

Dan released her hand. "That's it," he said encouragingly. "Keep going just like that."

Melanie tried to continue with what he had started, but she was so rattled she couldn't think straight. She dry-brushed blue all the way out into a wet patch of red, then inadvertently pulled red back halfway across her sky. She groaned, scrubbing furiously at the red streak in an attempt to blend it in.

"I like that," Dan announced, as if she had done it on purpose. He smiled at her again and almost—not quite—winked. "Interesting."

Interesting? If she wasn't interested in Dan, and he wasn't interested either, then why was he flirting with her?

He's not flirting with you, you nitwit. He's trying to teach you to paint.

Still . . . Melanie was no stranger to come-ons. Guys had been attracted to her all her life, and a certain percentage always felt as though they had to do something about it. She wasn't positive Dan was in that group yet, but she couldn't help wondering if he was so friendly with all his students.

"I, uh . . . I might as well add some yellow here, and try to make this more of a sunset," she said self-consciously. "I can overlap that red and get orange."

"Good idea," he said, nodding. "Give it a go."

She tried to read his expression, but got nothing. Whatever had passed between them seemed to have burned out as quickly as it had ignited. He appeared totally absorbed in painting again.

"Try pulling that yellow in from over here," he

suggested, pointing to a place at one edge of her canvas. "And maybe bring a streak of it across the grass. Let's not be so literal with our colors."

Melanie slapped paint around for a while, gradually relaxing. Whatever odd vibe she thought she had picked up on had totally disappeared.

Like he's really going to hit on you with Dad right downstairs anyway. How deluded can you be?

By the time her lesson was over, Melanie had almost forgotten the feel of Dan's fingers on hers. She managed to give him a fairly normal smile as he got ready to leave.

"I'll see you Sunday, then?" he asked, slinging his backpack over his shoulders.

The backpack made him look younger somehow, more like an eager boy—if boys could have rock-hard abs. Melanie tried not to notice the sliver of stomach where his pack had hitched up his shirt, but it was a wasted effort.

She was loyal to Jesse, but she was only human.

"Sunday," she agreed quickly, blushing as she walked him to the studio door. "Can you find your way out of here? I want to clean these brushes."

"Sure. No problem."

His grin was casual as he headed for the staircase. He didn't try to stay and chat her up. There was nothing at all in his manner to make her believe he had more than a professional interest in her.

Except that she did believe it. *Something* had passed between them. Some strange sort of chemistry . . .

Which is bad, she reminded herself, wheeling around and hurrying back into the studio. *Very, very bad. You're in love with Jesse, Dan's way too old for you, and he's probably as freaked out by whatever that just was as you are. A twenty-five-year-old with a fifteen-year-old? Never happen. I don't want it to happen.*

So why did a little voice keep telling her she could get him if she tried?

Six

"Well, this is boring," Gail announced, glancing scornfully around the mall. There were only a few scattered people in the interior courtyard that Thursday, mostly mothers with little kids. "Whose idea was it to come here?"

"Nicole's," Courtney said accusingly.

"Like there were so many other choices!" Nicole defended herself. "Why didn't we just go to Disney World? That's only a thousand miles away."

"Don't tempt me," Gail said, slouching against a column at the edge of the open area. "You're the one with the car—and the one whose parents'll call out the state troopers."

"It would be fun while it lasted, though," said Courtney, getting a faraway look in her eyes. "We'd be like Thelma and Louise . . . and someone."

"I'll be whichever one ended up with Brad Pitt," said Gail.

"No one ended up with Brad Pitt. They both ended up dead," Nicole told her, still annoyed.

Gail gave Courtney a mischievous smile. "It would almost be worth it, wouldn't it?"

"No kidding!" Courtney said, as if she had some basis for comparison.

Nicole glanced around to make sure no one was listening. It always irritated her when Courtney pretended to be more worldly than she was, but no matter how hard she tried, Courtney didn't have a prayer of keeping up with Gail. Luckily, the three of them were standing far enough out of the traffic pattern to prevent anyone from overhearing.

"If it's so boring here, let's leave," Nicole said, wishing she'd never cut another day of camp in the first place. She'd only agreed to hang out with Courtney and Gail because she hated worrying about what they were doing without her. *And because it bugs Mom.*

"Where do you want to go?" Gail asked, reaching into a pocket near the knee of her cargo pants. She was wearing them with a sports bra, their waistband riding so low that Nicole could see the lacy elastic of her cousin's underwear.

"I thought we were going to check out the guys in the arcade," Courtney whined.

Gail pulled a pack of cigarettes from her pocket, tapped one out, and lit up in one expert movement. "Want one?" she asked, offering the pack to Courtney.

Courtney shook her head.

"Well, I know Miss Goody Two-Shoes doesn't want one," Gail mocked, smiling a challenge at Nicole. "These things'll kill you, you know," she told Courtney.

"They will!" Nicole insisted, on the defensive again. She had given Gail plenty of grief about smoking when they were both working at Wienerageous. "Not to mention that they smell disgusting."

"Whatever." Gail blew out a lungful of smoke and flexed her bare torso from side to side. "They keep a girl thin."

"Really?"

Nicole's mother had smoked for years—and for that very reason—but now she swore that cigarettes did absolutely nothing for weight loss. Nicole and Heather had both heard a million times over how addictive cigarettes were and what complete misery quitting had been—and now Mrs. Brewster was the most militant antismoker Nicole knew. Nicole had always secretly wondered if her mom was telling the truth about the weight-loss part, or if she was only trying to keep her and Heather from picking up a bad habit.

"You don't hear me complaining about *my* weight, do you?" Gail replied, holding out the pack.

Nicole hesitated only long enough to make sure no one was watching before she grabbed a cigarette.

One isn't going to kill me, she thought. *And then I'll know the truth.*

Gail held out her lighter and flicked it with an evil grin. Nicole could tell her cousin thought she was corrupting her.

"What are you doing?" Courtney exclaimed, a trace of reluctant admiration in her voice. "You don't know how to smoke!"

"You breathe in, you breathe out," Nicole said tensely, not wanting them to know how scared she really was. "It isn't rocket science."

She stuck one end of the cigarette into her mouth and the other over Gail's lighter, inhaling quickly, before she could chicken out. Smoke burned down into her lungs, and the next moment she was coughing, each gasp releasing a puff of white.

"Smooth," Gail laughed. "No one would ever guess you hadn't done that before." She took a long drag off her own cigarette and blew a set of perfect smoke rings into the air-conditioned courtyard.

"I wasn't ready, that's all." Nicole's throat felt raw, but she wasn't sure if that was from the smoking or the coughing. Lifting the cigarette to her lips again, she took a second, more cautious puff.

"You smoke like a girl," Courtney criticized, imitating Nicole's stiffly spread fingers. "Or a Vulcan."

"Yeah," Gail jeered. "Live long and prosper."

At that moment, Nicole didn't feel likely to do either. Smoke filled her nose and lungs, reducing the amount of oxygen getting to her brain. Haze clung to her face like a film, and burning tobacco was all she could smell. She was actually getting dizzy, and a sudden wave of nausea brought her breakfast up in her throat.

I can see how these could make a person lose weight, she thought. The experience was incredibly unpleasant, but she definitely didn't feel like eating. She kept inhaling doggedly, watching with satisfaction as the end of the cigarette glowed red and burned itself shorter. It occurred to her that smokers usually took a lot more time between drags, but she wasn't enjoying herself enough to dawdle. Ignoring Courtney, Gail, and everything else in the mall, Nicole concentrated completely on the cigarette, her goal to finish it without coughing again.

"Nicole? What are you *doing?*" an amazed voice asked.

Startled, Nicole sucked down a lungful of smoke and immediately started wheezing. She gasped to recover herself, each exhalation a mini-foghorn.

"Lovely," said Noel, sneering slightly. "Nice habit."

He was as gorgeous as ever, his dark brown hair arranged in perfectly waxed spikes, a paper shopping bag dangling from one hand. He was wearing a short-sleeved madras shirt and sharply pressed khaki shorts with new sandals.

"Wh-what are you doing here?" Nicole finally got out, looking frantically for a place to ditch her cigarette. Gail's had disappeared like magic, despite the fact that there wasn't an ashtray or trash can in sight.

Desperate, Nicole held hers behind her back. Noel's raised eyebrows let her know she hadn't solved a thing.

"Since when do you smoke?" he asked.

"I don't. I mean, I was just—"

"Poor Nicole," Gail cut in, flashing Noel a way-too-flirtatious smile. "Someone told her that cigarettes would help her lose all that weight she's been gaining."

Nicole turned scarlet. The oxygen she hadn't been getting suddenly became an issue as the mall began spinning around her, Noel's disapproving face at the center of the vortex.

"So would pushing away from the feed trough," he said. "And that doesn't stink *or* give you cancer. Jeez, Nicole. Why not just try a little self-control?"

He walked away without waiting for a reply, without an introduction to Gail, without even letting Nicole recover her dignity.

"I'll call you," she bleated pathetically at his back. He didn't even turn his head.

Nicole turned pleadingly to Courtney, who gave her a sympathetic look, but Gail only laughed. "So, that's the boyfriend, huh? Thanks for introducing me."

"I think you made enough of an impression all on your own," Nicole returned angrily. "Thanks for stabbing me in the back!"

"Oh, please." Gail rolled her eyes. "It's not my fault

you let him sneak up on you. It's just common sense never to smoke in front of a guy you like until you find out if he smokes too." She moved one sneaker, exposing her own cigarette smashed flat against the floor.

So that's where she hid it. Nicole suppressed a surge of grudging admiration, wishing she'd had the presence of mind to do the same thing.

"Just call him tonight and tell him we dared you to smoke," Courtney said. "Tell him it was some sort of prank or . . . whatever. You'll think of something, and we'll back you up."

"Yeah. We'll back you up," Gail said, still staring in the direction Noel had disappeared.

"I don't need any more of *your* help," Nicole said sullenly.

Gail smiled. "Whatever you say."

And that was when Nicole realized something important: Her cousin had just told her that a smart girl never smokes in front of a guy she likes.

Gail's cigarette had been the first one out.

"I appreciate your meeting with me," Peter said nervously.

Jason's social worker, Valerie Horner, glanced at the clock on her desk. "Always happy to talk about one of my kids."

"Yeah. Well. Thanks."

Peter shifted uncomfortably in the chair she'd directed him to, hoping he didn't look too grungy after a full day at camp. He'd changed clothes at the cabin, but a swim in the lake had had to substitute for a shower. In order to get to the social worker's office before she left for the day, he'd had to skip the bus ride to the park and drive directly there from the lake.

"So what is it you wanted to talk about?" She glanced at her clock again, then raised an eyebrow at him.

"About Jason's adoption."

Ms. Horner's eyes narrowed. "Who told you he was going to be adopted?"

"He did. He knows he's being put up for adoption, and he's really worried about it."

"Oh. That's all right, then," she said, nodding. "There are confidentiality issues with this sort of thing, but we can't stop the children from talking about themselves. I wish we could sometimes. They blurt out the most inappropriate things to total strangers."

"I'm not a stranger," Peter said. "I've known Jason ever since he went into foster care—about two years now."

The woman referred to some notes on her desk. "Right. You run some sort of Saturday program he's in?"

"During the school year. This summer he's in day camp with me all week."

"So you think you know him pretty well."

"I *do* know him pretty well. And I'd like to help you find him a home."

"Excuse me?" Ms. Horner leaned back in her chair, an amused expression on her face. "Any particular home in mind?"

"No. I just thought that maybe if you had some help, you could find someplace faster and put the poor kid out of his misery. Jason probably acts pretty tough when he talks to you, but I see him every day, and he's barely even himself anymore. The stress is changing his entire personality."

"Look . . . Peter, is it? I'm sure you mean well, but adoption is a complicated process, full of laws and regulations, and that's why the government hires professionals like me to look out for kids like Jason. As much as we might like the process to move faster sometimes, there are ways to do these things. And I know what they are."

Had he offended her somehow? She seemed awfully touchy all of a sudden.

"Of course," he said quickly. "It's just that I know once kids reach Jason's age, it gets hard to find adoptive homes for them. And Jason doesn't exactly have the cleanest track record when it comes to staying out of trouble. But deep down he's a good kid. I know he would be a good son, if someone just gave him a chance." Peter smiled ruefully. "Or maybe two or three."

"I'm not sure what you're saying. You want to be an advocate for Jason?"

"Yes! An advocate!" he agreed, seizing on her word. "I was thinking maybe I could put together some sort of information sheet about Jason, with his picture and what he likes to do and everything, and pass it out at my church. Then people could call me if they have any questions and I can tell them what a great kid he is."

"Oh, no. I can't allow that." Ms. Horner sat up straight in her chair, her eyebrows drawing together. "There are strict privacy issues. I can't have you passing Jason's picture around like a lost dog's."

"It wouldn't be that way!" Peter protested. "I'd just give the flyers to people I know. I'm not going to staple his face to telephone poles."

"No. I'm sorry," she said firmly. "In fact, I have to ask you not to speak about Jason to other people at all. You have to respect the law and let us do our job."

"I can't even talk to my own friends about him?" Peter said. "People my family might know?"

"Well . . ." Ms. Horner took a long time with her answer. "I suppose that would be all right. As long as you don't tell them anything personal about Jason."

Huh? How was he supposed to talk Jason up if he wasn't allowed to talk about him? Did the woman even realize she was speaking out of both sides of her mouth?

"Don't forget there are other parties to consider. Jason's parents—"

x

85

"Didn't even care enough to get him back!" Peter interrupted, his frustration making him angry. "You're worried about *their* privacy? What for?"

"See? Now that's why this is a job for professionals. Sometimes it's better if you're not too close to these things."

Not too close? Peter couldn't believe his ears. *Somebody* needs *to be close!*

Was Ms. Horner really telling him that a bunch of regulations and the rights of Jason's parents were more important than Jason's future? Than Jason's life?

She rose from her desk abruptly, signaling the end of the meeting. "Thanks for stopping by, Peter. I appreciate your concern for Jason."

He hated the way she kept saying Jason's name— as if she and Jason were such good buddies when she only saw him for an hour each month—but somehow he managed to keep his disgust off his face. If he was going to help Jason, he might have to deal with Valerie Horner again, and it definitely wouldn't pay to make her an enemy. If she wanted to, she could yank Jason out of camp, out of Junior Explorers, and out of Peter's life completely.

"I am concerned for Jason," Peter said carefully. "And I know you are too. If there's anything I can do to help things along in any way . . ."

"Right. Right, I know where you are," she said, hustling him out the door.

* * *

"I just think we should have more quiet, *romantic* songs," Jenna insisted at band practice Thursday night. "I'm sorry, but some of the songs on that list aren't good wedding songs at all."

She pointed to the sheet of paper nailed up inside Guy Vaughn's garage—the playlist Trinity was currently working on learning.

"We all agreed to that list," Evan said tersely, setting his bass in its case on the floor. "You agreed to it too."

"I agreed to it in *general*!" she said, exasperated. "Not as a blueprint for my own sister's wedding!"

"The list is the list." Paul hit a cymbal for emphasis. "We didn't say we were going to have a different list for every wedding."

"Not for *every* wedding." Jenna squeezed her eyes shut, wondering if the concept was really so hard to grasp or if they were just being dense on purpose. Evan and Paul *liked* all that underground, no-normal-person-has-ever-heard-it-before stuff, but she didn't. If they wanted to play those songs at some stranger's wedding, fine. But not at Caitlin's.

"The thing is, Jenna," Guy intervened, "those songs are the only ones we know. Those are the only ones we've been practicing. And your sister's wedding isn't that far away."

"Exactly! Which is why I'm saying let's forget about some of those for now and learn these others instead."

She waved a stack of sheet music, purchased with

her own allowance after camp that afternoon. They should have been appreciative, since every song she'd picked was perfect for any other wedding they'd ever work, but instead she was getting attitude.

"What you're saying is, you want to choose the whole playlist," Evan corrected sullenly.

"That's not true! But even if it were, would that be so wrong? You guys wanted a wedding, and I got us a wedding. I ought to have some say-so about the music for my own sister."

"Except that this isn't just for your sister," Paul said. "We're hoping to get other jobs off this."

"Caitlin's still the customer, so she should get what she wants."

"The customer?" Evan retorted. "She's not even paying us!"

"All right," Guy broke in. "This isn't getting us anywhere. How many new songs do you have there, Jenna?"

"Five. Or six."

Or seven, she added silently.

"It shouldn't be that hard to learn songs we have sheet music for," Guy told Paul and Evan. "Maybe we just run through them a few times, and when we play them at the wedding we read them off the music. We don't have to memorize anything."

"Truuuuue," Paul said slowly.

"Although we might as well," Jenna interjected.

"They're all good songs. I'm sure we'll use them over and over."

Guy gave her an irritated look. "But we don't *have* to memorize them," he repeated for the guys, a note of warning in his voice.

Jenna didn't want to make the band angry; she only wanted her way. "Suit yourselves," she said with a shrug. "Just so long as we play them."

If Guy wanted to baby Evan and Paul, that was his business.

What got played at her sister's wedding was hers.

Seven

"When should I pick you up for the party?" Miguel asked, pulling to a stop at the curb in front of the Rosenthals' condominium building. "Or do you want to drive tonight?"

Leah sat forward to get out of his car and nearly yelped with pain. The halter she'd worn to camp that day had allowed her bare back to fuse to the vinyl passenger seat, and she had just ripped herself halfway free.

"Ow, ow, ow," she whimpered, peeling herself off the rest of the way as if her back were an open wound and the seat a giant Band-Aid. "Ow, that really hurts."

She tried to twist around to see the damage, but Miguel caught her by the shoulders, turning her back toward him.

"You are *sunburned*!" he said. "You wouldn't believe how red your back is right now."

"I might." She winced as she removed his fingers from her shoulders. Each one left a white mark where the pressure had been, marks which quickly filled with scarlet to match the rest of her skin.

"I've never seen you burn this way," he said. "You don't usually burn at all."

Leah shrugged. She didn't usually wear a backless top all day in the sun either. And she usually wore sunscreen. But that day she had decided she needed an extra-deep tan for the new dress she planned to wear to the party at Mitch Powell's house. A lot of people were going to be there, and Leah wanted to make sure Miguel had eyes for no one but her. They'd go to the party, do a little dancing, and afterward she'd bring him back to the condo. Now that she'd had more time to think about it, there was no way she was going to drop the subject of sex where they'd left it during their last discussion. She needed to know where she stood with him; he couldn't just brush her off the way he had and then blame it on his church. Besides, now that he'd had a couple of days to stew about her offer, he might be seeing things in a whole new light. . . .

"That can't feel good," he said, pressing a finger into her back. "Maybe we ought to skip the party tonight."

"No!" she exclaimed. "No, I'll be fine. I'll just take a nice cool bath, maybe with some of that leftover oatmeal stuff from the poison ivy. . . ."

Miguel laughed. "You're giving that tub a workout this week."

"I know." At least her poison ivy was finally on the way out. Not only did it no longer itch, the rash had healed to the point where it was barely noticeable.

"All right. Why don't you call me when you're ready to go? We'll figure out who's driving then."

They said their good-byes, Leah trying not to flinch when he hugged her. Her sunburn was hurting more by the second, but she didn't want him to know that. The night ahead of them was too important to let a little scorching get in the way.

This is the night we set everything straight, she thought. *I'll bet there's a big difference between what he says and what he really wants. Tonight is the night I find out!*

Riding up the elevator to the condo, though, she started feeling sick. The little elevator car was so hot and stuffy that the walls seemed to be closing in. She was practically gasping for breath by the time she burst out on her floor.

I just need to cool off, she thought, stumbling through her front door and heading straight for the bathtub. She was filling it with cold water when the telephone rang. Grabbing the cordless, she hurried back into the bathroom to make sure the tub didn't overflow.

"Hi!" her mother said on the line. "How's everything going? Are you having fun? Do you miss us?"

Leah laughed. "Fine, yes, and yes. How's the antiquing? Find anything good yet?"

"Oh, tons of things. Your father's already complaining that we're going to have to buy a bigger place when we get back."

Leah smiled, imagining the grumbling.

"But how are *you*?" her mother asked. "I would

92

have called before, but your father keeps saying you're a big girl now and don't need us checking up on you every minute. How is it checking up to say hello to my own daughter?"

"I'm fine," Leah reassured her. "Well, a little sunburned, but otherwise fine."

"Sunburned?" her mother repeated, concerned. "You don't usually burn. Did you wear sunscreen?"

"It's nothing," Leah said, wishing she hadn't mentioned it. "I'm just about to take a cold bath."

"I thought I heard water running. Is your skin that bad?"

"No," she lied, twisting around to see her back in the bathroom mirror. She pulled the string at the top of her halter, allowing the shirt to fall to her waist. Where the bow had been tied at her neck, a perfect pale replica remained on her red skin, crooked loops and all.

"You should take it easy tonight," her mother recommended. "Slather up with aloe, put on a nice loose bathrobe, and watch a TV movie or something."

That sounded surprisingly tempting. Leah eased herself down into the water, half wishing she hadn't already made other plans.

"Miguel and I are going to a party tonight."

"He won't expect you to go if you're sunburned!"

"He doesn't *expect* me to go, Mom. I want to."

But after Leah got off the phone, after she'd spent nearly an hour soaking in unpleasantly cool water, she felt less like going to a party than she ever had in her life. Despite her shivering, her back was still on fire, so much so that she could barely stand to blot it with a towel. She checked the mirror again, hoping to see an improvement, but her burn looked even worse.

"I can't believe I did this to myself. Especially today," she groaned.

She could never wear her new dress to the party now, not the way it laced across her bare back. She'd be in agony the whole night. Not to mention that she was suddenly feeling kind of nauseous . . .

I need to lie down. The blood pounded in her ears as she headed for her bedroom. Collapsing gratefully onto the cool bedspread, she stretched out with nothing but the damp towel draped over her.

She couldn't remember ever having been so sunburned before, not even when she was a little kid. *Especially not when I was a kid*, she thought wryly. *Mom would have a heart attack if she saw my back right now.*

In her mind she saw a string of childhood swimsuits and her mother constantly hovering on the periphery of the action, the ever-present bottle of sunscreen in her hand. Leah had complained vociferously about the relentless slatherings, but her mother had always said the same thing: "You'll thank me someday."

I would have thanked you today, Leah realized, suddenly overcome with missing her mother. Her parents had been gone for a week, and while she'd been aware of their absence, she couldn't say she had truly missed them before that moment. Now she missed them terribly.

If Mom were home, she'd bring me some aspirin, make me a milkshake, and put cold cloths on my back. Dad would tease me for being so dumb; then he'd make five trips to the store to get aloe vera gel, and ice cream, and whatever else he could think of.

A tear squeezed out and ran onto her pillows, and Leah wasn't even sure why she was crying. It could have been because her back hurt, or because she was mad at herself for being so stupid, or, perhaps most likely of all, because she was just starting to realize what life without her mom and dad would be like. It made her sad to think she could have gone with them instead of staying home with Miguel. Not that she *regretted* staying. Not exactly. She just hated to think that maybe her parents didn't know how much she loved them. No matter how she changed, she would always be their little girl.

By the time the telephone rang again, her pillow was nearly as wet as her towel.

"I thought you were going to call me," said Miguel.

"I was." Leah sniffed hard against a headful of tears. "You said to call you when I was ready, and I'm not ready yet."

"Have you been *crying?*"

"No." She sniffed again. "A little," she admitted.

"What for? What's the matter?"

She wanted to tell him. That growing up was harder than she'd expected, that she was going to miss her parents and Clearwater Crossing so much, that she was suddenly having second thoughts about how far to push things that night . . .

"I don't feel very well," she said, settling on the easiest excuse. "My back really hurts and I'm hot all over and—"

"Then let's forget about the party! You should take it easy, and I don't have to go. There's always plenty to do around here."

"Stripping woodwork isn't exactly a thrilling Friday night," she protested.

He chuckled. "You'd be surprised."

"You really don't mind if we don't go?"

"Nah. I'll miss you, but it's no big deal."

Part of her felt as though she ought to be offended that he would give up on her so easily.

Most of her was just relieved.

"Call me tomorrow," she said, hanging up before she could start crying again. Her tears returned the very next moment.

What is my problem? she wondered, sitting up to wipe her face with the towel. As emotional as she was all of a sudden, she was glad she wasn't going to the party. She was glad Miguel hadn't suggested that he come to her place instead. And she was incredibly glad she wouldn't be attempting a seduction in the next few hours.

All I really want tonight is a bowl of ice cream and a sofa all to myself.

"I, uh, I heard there's an open party tonight," Bernie said shyly as Ben let her into his mother's car. She was wearing a close-fitting pink sundress with narrow shoulder straps. Pink rhinestone clips glittered in her short brown hair. "Some guy named Mitch. Do you know him?"

Ben froze. He had heard about the party from Eight Prime, but he hadn't planned on going. He certainly hadn't expected *Bernie* to know about it. Slowly he released the passenger door handle and assumed what he hoped was a casual stance on the curb.

"Mitch Powell? Yeah, I know him. The guy's a jerk."

Ben couldn't stand Powell and his brainless best friend, Whitey Wallace. Between constantly bullying him and giving him the particularly annoying nickname of Pimple, those two had made his gym class a living hell.

"Well, but . . . we don't have to talk to him, do we?" Bernie asked. "I just thought maybe . . . my first high school party . . ."

Mitch and Whitey had laid off him later in the year, once they'd figured out he was in tight with some popular people, but Ben still couldn't take the chance. The last thing he wanted was for one of those fools to call him Pimple in front of Bernie.

"It's just that this movie is supposed to be really

good," he said, handing her the ad he'd cut from the paper. "Melanie and Jesse liked it."

Melanie and Jesse were the ultimate cool couple, so anything they liked had to be good. On the other hand, Ben was pretty sure Melanie and Jesse were going to Mitch's party too—and he definitely didn't plan to mention that.

Bernie shrugged. "Okay."

Ben breathed a sigh of relief. "Okay!"

He hurried around to the driver's seat and quickly pulled out onto the street, wanting to get to the theater. Once he bought the movie tickets, there could be no change of plans.

"You look nice," he told her as he drove, hoping for a smile. She didn't disappoint him, although she still looked a little wistful.

"Is that a new dress?" he asked. "I like it."

"Kind of. I've had it, but I was saving it for something special."

Ben couldn't help beaming at the realization that Bernie thought a date with him was special enough to break out a new dress. *I'll make it up to her about missing the party,* he vowed. *Besides, it's not like we planned to go there.*

"How about after the movie we go to The Danger Zone?" he suggested. "We can get a pizza and play some arcade games. It ought to be pretty busy on a Friday night—way more fun than Powell's stupid party."

"All right," she said good-naturedly. "Besides, we'll be going to plenty of cool parties once school starts."

"We will?" he said, taken by surprise. "No! I mean . . . right! We will!"

Most CCHS parties were open anyway, and he had Eight Prime to let him know where the cool ones were taking place. As long as he and Bernie kept to the sidelines, he could probably avoid harassment. Maybe.

He could try.

Of course, that assumes Bernie still likes me in the fall. Which isn't too likely the way things are going.

He could feel his hands growing slick on the wheel as he drove through the quiet streets. Mrs. Pipkin was determined to continue her program at Slenderific Studios; Ben's hints about simply dieting on her own had fallen on deaf ears. The only other method he'd been able to think of for keeping her and Bernie apart was to get Bernie to quit her job somehow. Considering that she wasn't even officially in high school yet and she was already getting paid to work with computers, that didn't seem very likely.

Still . . . you never know unless you try.

"So. How are things going at your new job?" he asked. "Getting bored yet?"

Her eyes went round with surprise. "Bored! This is like the best thing I ever—" She stopped talking abruptly, visibly quenching her enthusiasm. "I mean, it's all right. Not that hard."

99

Ben had a feeling Bernie understood a lot more about computers than she let on, but he wasn't sure why. She never wanted to go into any detail about whatever programming she was doing.

Maybe she thinks I won't understand it, he concluded ironically.

"It must get kind of old, though," he insisted. "Just entering data all day."

"I don't mind."

"But it's summertime! Wouldn't you rather be outside?"

She chuckled a little nervously. "You sound like you're trying to talk me out of working."

"Not at all!" he lied. "I'm only saying, it's not like you *have* to work."

"Actually? It kind of is." She looked down at her lap, clearly embarrassed. "My mom works really hard, but when all the bills are paid, there's not a lot left over. She said if I got a summer job, I could spend all the money I made on clothes and . . . well, whatever I want."

Like maybe a new computer, he thought. Bernie wouldn't say so, but he was pretty sure the reason she spent so much time in the computer lab at the library was that she didn't have a computer at home.

So it's hopeless. If a summer job was *his* only way of getting a computer, Ben knew he wouldn't quit even a bad job—and Bernie had a good one.

Mom's not going to quit her diet. And Bernie's not go-

ing to quit working. *And that means sooner or later the two of them are bound to run into each other.*

His hands started slipping on the wheel again. He glanced over at Bernie, heartsick at the thought of losing her.

There's got to be some way of keeping them apart. What I need here is a plan!

Eight

"So what are we doing today?" Jenna asked Caitlin Saturday morning. The sun was already streaming between the open lilac curtains of their third-floor bedroom window, promising a perfect summer day. "This would be a good day to order the cake."

Caitlin shook her head. "I don't want to do that so far ahead. The wedding's still over a month away."

She pulled on a lightweight cotton dress and began buttoning it up the front. Strappy, backless dresses were the rage in Clearwater Crossing that July, but Caitlin's had short sleeves and a full flowing skirt that skimmed her calves just above her ankles. She looked both sweet and old-fashioned . . . exactly like herself.

"They're not going to *make* the cake today," Jenna said. "We just need to *order* it now, so we get on the schedule. It would be horrible if we waited so long that we couldn't get one."

"Between our whole family, we'd figure it out." Caitlin added a flat straw hat to her outfit, a silk

102

sunflower on its front echoing the tiny daisies on her dress. "We could make cupcakes, for that matter. That would be kind of fun, in fact—a cupcake for each of the guests."

"I've never seen that done," Jenna said, which was all the reason she needed for dismissing the idea out of hand. "Besides, what about the cake top? You can't have a cake top on cupcakes."

Caitlin smiled. "Good. One less decision for me."

"And you can't cut a cupcake either. How are you going to do a cake cutting with cupcakes?"

"I don't know, Jenna. I just don't want to think about cake today, all right?"

It wasn't all right, but it wasn't as if they didn't have a lot of other stuff they could figure out instead.

"What about the menu, then?" Still in her pajamas, Jenna got up off her bed and fetched her steno pad from her desk. Flipping to a full page, she tried to show it to Caitlin.

"What's that?" Caitlin's attention was on the mirror as she took off her hat and rearranged her light brown hair.

"A bunch of different appetizers and main course ideas. But you have to pick a caterer, Caitlin. It doesn't make a lot of sense for me to keep making up menus when all these people are going to have their own."

"Don't do it, then," Caitlin said simply.

103

"I *have* to! Somebody has to, anyway. Do you want to go talk to caterers today? See who you like?"

Caitlin shook her head. "I'm meeting David in fifteen minutes."

Jenna could barely believe her ears. "*Again?* When are you going to be back?"

"Not until late. Don't wait up."

"But Caitlin! We have all this stuff to do! Not just the cake and the caterer. There's the flowers, and the invitations, and—"

"Mom's taking care of the invitations."

"She is? How come nobody told me?"

"And as far as everything else goes, it's either under control, or I don't feel like thinking about it right now. I'm not going to waste such a beautiful day on chores and errands when I can be spending it with David. Have fun. I'll see you later."

She made a hurried exit, leaving Jenna gaping. Her sister thought planning the most important day of her life was "chores and errands"? Was she *crazy*? Jenna stared at the doorway Caitlin had just walked through, expecting her to return any second. Then the front door slammed and Jenna knew she was really gone.

"This is terrible!" she groaned, falling backward on her bed. She was never going to get the wedding planned at this rate. Not only that, but she hadn't made plans with any of her friends because she had expected to spend the entire day helping Caitlin.

Now Cat had left her high and dry.

What are she and David doing today that's so all-fired important anyway? Jenna wondered grumpily.

One possible answer brought her bolt upright on her bed, heart pounding.

Are they making plans without me?

After all, the wedding had to get planned sometime, and Caitlin definitely hadn't been doing anything about it with Jenna the last few days. If she didn't mind going behind Jenna's back on the invitations, who knew what else she might be up to? She and David could be on their way to choose tuxes that very minute, or off looking at reception halls, or . . .

"Mom!" Jenna yelled, running down the stairs.

If Caitlin was cutting her out of the loop, she definitely wanted to know about it.

"What do you think of Rebecca?" Nicole's mother asked. "I always thought that was a pretty name."

Nicole shrugged.

"What does it mean?" Heather asked, grabbing for one of the baby name books to look it up. Mr. Brewster had gone in for some extra hours at work that Saturday, leaving the three female members of his family still sitting around the breakfast table. "Captivating!" Heather announced.

"I've always liked that name," Mrs. Brewster said. "It is pretty, isn't it, Nicole?"

Nicole tossed her head, annoyed by being dragged

into yet another discussion about the baby. "I hope you like Becky, too, because that's what everyone will call her."

"Or Becca," Heather piped up. "Becca is pretty."

"Why not just Rebecca?" Mrs. Brewster demanded.

"Three syllables. Never happen." Nicole reached for another slice of bacon. She had already eaten six, and two eggs cooked in bacon grease, but she still didn't feel satisfied. For the last two days she had been on a new no-carbohydrate diet, and while she was already pining for bread and potatoes and chips and sweets, at least on this plan she got to eat.

"I like Mariah," Heather volunteered. "Mariah Brewster."

Nicole actually kind of liked Mariah, but she wrinkled her nose at the sound of her own completely unromantic last name. "If she's lucky, she'll marry young and take her husband's name."

"What if it's a boy?" her mother asked.

"Then he's screwed."

"Nicole!"

"What?" Was it *her* fault they were all named Brewster?

"That's not a nice expression," said her mother. "Not to mention how disrespectful it is to your father." She pushed back from the table, her belly jutting into her lap. "Anyway, we have plenty of time to think of names. What we need to do today is get that

106

sewing room emptied out and painted. Since you girls are both home, you can help me."

"No fair!" Nicole cried. "If I'd known that, I would have made plans!"

Her mother gave her a blistering look. "I'm getting tired of your attitude, Princess. Now march upstairs, get dressed, and be in the baby's room in five minutes."

Nicole bolted from the dining room table, tears burning her eyes. Her life was a disaster! Courtney and Gail were so tight now she felt like a third wheel, Noel had been totally aloof when she'd called him after that smoking fiasco in the mall, and her family life . . .

. . . *has never been worse*, she concluded as she ran up the stairs, a state of affairs that she would have considered impossible a year ago. She and Heather had always hated each other, had always fought over trivial things, but Nicole had at least resigned herself to her sister's presence. That was more than she could say about the baby's.

Grabbing some dirty clothes off her bedroom chair, Nicole dressed hurriedly, not in the least concerned about how she looked. In the bathroom, she splashed cold water on her face and tried to compose herself. If she had to do her mother's grunt work, at least she didn't have to let her know how much it bothered her.

"Nice of you to join us," her mother said when Nicole slunk into the sewing room ten minutes later.

"Whatever," Nicole muttered.

To call the Brewsters' closet of a junk room the sewing room was simply another example of her mother's optimism. A small, square window was centered over a battered chest in the narrow wall across from the door. A long folding table dominated one side wall, the sewing machine at its center all but buried beneath piles of fabric, boxes of papers, discarded games, and clothes that needed mending. The opposite wall held a dresser piled high with more boxes, and a sprung, dusty chair that Mrs. Brewster had bought at a garage sale and never refinished. A small closet on the same wall as the door was packed to the ceiling with things that had been too good to throw out but not good enough to ever use again.

Mrs. Brewster rolled up the blackout blind. It spun recklessly when she let it go.

"I'll definitely be taking that down," she said, a disapproving look on her face. "The room is too small for curtains, though, so I guess I'll get a nice miniblind."

"What about shutters?" Heather suggested. "Shutters are good."

"Shutters *are* good," Mrs. Brewster said thoughtfully.

Nicole rolled her eyes. "Are we working, or are we going to stand around yakking all day?"

"Fine," her mother snapped. "You can start by taking all of this stuff down to the garage. Your father set up some shelves in there. Make sure you stack things *neatly.*"

Nicole grabbed a box and headed silently for the stairs, with Heather right behind her.

Only a hundred more trips to go, she thought sullenly as she shoved the box onto a shelf in the garage. Her mother wasn't helping, of course; she was far too delicate to carry her own junk. Nicole found her folding old clothes when she went back for seconds and sorting through the closet when she went back for thirds. She lost track of how many trips she'd made before the closet was finally empty and the room down to bare furniture. Mrs. Brewster had managed to get the sewing machine into its case by then and was struggling with the folding table.

"Almost ready to paint!" she said cheerfully, as if she had had something to do with that.

Sweating now, Nicole walked past her to open the small window. It was even hotter outside than in, but at least a slight breeze was blowing. Nicole stood with her nose to the screen, breathing in the fresh air. When she turned around at last, her mother was standing right behind her.

"Do I smell *cigarettes?*" Mrs. Brewster demanded.

"What? No!" Nicole hadn't smoked since that one stupid attempt on Thursday, and considering how poorly that had gone, she didn't intend to try again.

Her mother came closer and sniffed her hair. "Something reeks," she insisted.

With a start, Nicole realized she was wearing the same dirty shirt she'd had on in the mall Thursday. And suddenly she smelled what her mom was talking about.

The smoke must be down in the fabric. Then, when I started sweating . . .

"This is a dirty shirt, that's all," she blurted out, terrified of being caught.

Mrs. Brewster fixed her with suspiciously narrowed eyes. "That had *better* be all. Because you know I'd have to kill you if I ever caught you smoking."

"I know." Boy, did she know. She didn't even want to think about that.

"Go put on something to paint in, and drop those stinky clothes in the wash," her mother told her.

"Like what?" Nicole asked. "I don't have any clothes I want to ruin."

"Overalls!" said Heather. "I'll go put mine on." She ran out of the room.

"I don't *have* any overalls," Nicole complained, seeing a potential way out of the afternoon's work.

"It doesn't have to be overalls."

"*Heather* has overalls," she whined.

Her mother glanced impatiently at her watch. "Fine. Run over to the church secondhand store and get some. But hurry up—I'm timing you."

I'm timing you, Nicole mocked bitterly as she pulled

110

her mother's car into the parking lot at the second-hand store. At least she was out of the house, though. And she seemed to have gotten off the hook about the cigarettes.

I'm not even going to hang around Gail when she smokes anymore, Nicole thought, walking into the store and beginning to look through a rack of denim. *Mom has a nose like a bloodhound.*

She eventually located a pair of overalls and held them against her body. They were too big, too plain, and probably men's, but she didn't care.

It's not like I want secondhand overalls, she thought, pulling them on over her shorts and snapping the shoulder straps. *This is purely about stalling Mom.*

There was a full-length mirror at the front of the store. Nicole threaded her way over, expecting to be appalled by her reflection.

On the contrary! she thought, dropping her purse in surprise. The overalls themselves were awful—faded, baggy, and thin in the knees—but they made her figure look great.

They're like a miracle, she thought disbelievingly, turning to view herself from all sides. *They hide everything!*

Something about the oversized nature of the garment made the parts of her body still showing look impressively thin, as if benefiting from the contrast.

Oh, I'm definitely buying these, Nicole thought,

picking up her purse. *I'd take a pair of these in every color they have!*

"I just don't think they get it," Peter complained to his parents during dinner Saturday night. There were only the three of them at the table, David being out with Caitlin again. "I mean, I know they're the professionals, but what are they doing? Not one thing."

"That you know of," his mother corrected mildly. "These things take time."

"They take too *much* time! That's my point."

Peter's dad smiled sympathetically and passed Peter the dinner rolls. "How's Jason doing?" he asked.

"Not good."

Peter ripped a roll apart, thinking about the past week at camp. Even though he had gotten Jason permission to go on the overnight and had already set him up with one of his own sleeping bags, the boy remained sullen and distant, not himself at all. The poor kid was simply going through the motions, waiting for strangers to decide his fate.

Waiting is the key word, Peter thought disgustedly, setting the untasted roll on his plate.

"Is he still misbehaving?" Mrs. Altmann asked.

Peter shook his head. "Not so much. It's like he doesn't even have the energy to get into trouble anymore. I'm telling you, he's just coming apart day by day. Somebody needs to *do* something."

"You're doing all you can . . . ," Mr. Altmann began.

"It's not enough!" Peter exploded, his emotions getting the better of him. "What are the so-called adults doing? If someone would just take Jason in hand, give him some love and stability . . . that's all he needs. He's a good kid. He really is."

Peter's mother reached across the table and put her hand on his. "Don't sell yourself short. I know you're frustrated, but what you're giving Jason is worth a lot."

Peter stared down at his barely touched pot roast and shook his head, angry tears in his eyes. He wasn't enough, and he never could be. Jason needed a father.

"Listen," his mother continued. "You know Jason is welcome here anytime. Why don't you bring him by? He could come for dinner, or just to hang out. We could make cookies or whatever you want. Okay?"

Peter nodded mutely, a lump in his throat.

"Good idea, son," Mr. Altmann said. "You know what else? There's a bunch of scrap lumber out in the garage. If we picked up some wheels somewhere, we could build a go-cart with Jason. Remember that old go-cart you and David used to have? You kids pushed that thing all over the neighborhood."

Peter nodded again, the lump practically choking him now. All he wanted for Jason were the same things he'd had himself: a regular home, loving parents, maybe a brother or two.

Just a normal childhood with normal people.

Was that too much to ask?

Nine

"Congratulate me," Ben's mom told him at Sunday breakfast. "I've lost five pounds!"

"Already? Wow, that's great!" he said sincerely.

"I can't wait to weigh in at Slenderific Studios this morning."

Ben almost choked on his toast. "*This* morning?"

Bernie was working at the clinic. He knew, because she'd already turned him down for a bike ride through the park.

"It's been a week."

"No, tomorrow!" he said anxiously. "*Tomorrow* is a week."

His mother shrugged. "I think it will be more fun to go on the weekends. They're supposed to have a big group there on Sundays."

That's what I'm afraid of, he thought, pushing his plate away.

Still . . . after two sleepless nights he *had* come up with a plan for a situation like this.

It just wasn't a very good one.

"I'll drive you!" he volunteered quickly. "What time are you supposed to be there?"

His mom checked her watch. "In half an hour."

Ben pushed back from the table. "I'll go warm up the car."

"It's only a five-minute drive," she said. "I don't think it needs to warm up twenty-five minutes."

"No. But I'll, uh . . . I'll take it over to the gas station and check the oil and water."

"You can do that in the driveway," his mother protested, but Ben was already charging for the garage.

"Be right back!" he shouted, knowing he had to move fast.

Bernie was entering data that day, but from what he'd been able to gather, she wasn't on any rigid schedule. So long as she got the work done, she could come and go as she pleased.

I'll just have to make sure she goes, he thought, doing a superhero-style leap into his mother's car.

The five-minute drive to the weight-loss clinic seemed to take an hour. Ben watched the dashboard clock more than the road as he raced through the downtown streets, screeching to a halt at the curb in front of the building. He ran into Slenderific Studios, spotted Bernie working at a desk, and darted behind the reception counter to grab her by one arm.

"Come on," he said frantically, pulling her to her feet. "We have to go."

"Go?" Bernie glanced nervously from him to the receptionist he had just barged past. "Go where?"

"I'll tell you in the car. Come on, I'm parked right outside." He dragged her to the doorway, ignoring her protests.

"Just a little emergency," he explained, flashing the openly staring woman behind the counter a fake smile. "We'll clear this up, and be back soon."

"What emergency?" Bernie asked as he pulled her to the curb and practically stuffed her into the car. "What's going on?"

"Tell you in a second."

Running around to the driver's side, he jumped in, and pulled the car out into traffic. "I'm taking you to breakfast," he announced.

"*What?* Ben, I was *working*."

"I'll bet they don't have Belgian waffles at Slenderific Studios."

"Of course they don't—it's a *diet* studio."

"You know where they have great ones? Connie's Corner. Let's go."

"I can't!" she protested.

"Of course you can. We'll just have some breakfast, then I'll drive you straight back. Come on, Bernie. It'll be fun."

She hesitated, then smiled, showing small white teeth. "All right," she said, giving in. "I've missed you."

Ben's heart flip-flopped like a beached fish. "I

missed you, too." No matter what he had to go through now to keep his mother and Bernie apart, it was worth it.

Parking in front of the coffee shop, he hustled her inside, sighing with relief when the hostess seated them right away.

"What are you going to have?" he asked, talking on before Bernie could answer. "The waffles are the best. I'm going to have the waffles. You should have the waffles. I'm going to use the men's room."

He was up and running for the back of the restaurant the next second, bursting though the door into the alley. A quick jog around the block and he was back in his mother's car, steering wildly for home.

I can be back at the restaurant in ten minutes, he thought, praying his mother would be ready to leave when he got there. He'd drop her off behind the clinic again, so that the nosy receptionist didn't see him. Then he'd park in front of the restaurant, run around to the back door, and tell Bernie there was a line to use the toilet.

A long *line*, he amended, refusing to think about how embarrassing that would be. *Bernie's worth it.*

He pulled into his own driveway and leaned on the horn, cringing at his mother's expression when she came out a moment later.

"Do *not* do that again!" she said, glancing up and

down the street as if expecting all the neighbors to come running. "It's very inconsiderate."

"Sorry," he muttered, leaning across to push the passenger door open. "I just don't want you to be late."

"Then you shouldn't have stayed so long at the gas station," Mrs. Pipkin replied, taking her time getting in. Ben peeled out of the driveway while she was still buckling her seat belt, ignoring the dirty look she gave him.

"You're driving too fast, Benny."

"No, right at the speed limit," he lied, easing off the accelerator.

"You're acting very strange this morning."

"What? No I'm not."

"Yes. You are."

He was off-loading her in the clinic's parking lot before she could elaborate. "See you in an hour!" he called, rocketing back toward the coffee shop.

Bernie was still at the table where he had left her, looking very put out.

"Where have you been?" she cried. "The waitress has been here five times!"

"I was, uh, in the bathroom," he said, feeling the blush burn up his cheeks. "There was a really long line."

"Who was in it?" she asked, gesturing around the restaurant. "There's practically no one here."

Oops. Why hadn't he thought of that? *I could say I was sitting on the toilet all this time—except she'd probably be so grossed out she'd never want to see me again.*

"It was just . . . they all went out the back door." Catching the waitress's eye, Ben waved her over frantically.

That was close, he thought as Bernie ordered her waffles. *And how will I get her to wait that long again while I go pick up Mom and drop her at home? I'm going to have to say I'm sick or something.*

Ben ordered the same thing as Bernie. Since it was his idea to come to breakfast, he couldn't very well tell her he'd just eaten.

"So, why are we here?" Bernie asked when the waitress had gone. "Why this sudden, burning urge for waffles?"

"Spontaneity!" he blurted out, saying the first thing that came into his head. "A romance fizzles without spontaneity."

Bernie smiled shyly, her eyes dropping to her scalloped paper place mat. "Is that what we have? A romance?"

The hopeful way she asked it nearly took his breath away.

"We will," he promised, for himself as much as for her. Whatever he had to do, whatever lame plans he had to put into action . . . it was all worth it to keep Bernie thinking he was worthy of her.

Except that you're not, a little voice inside his head mocked. *And sooner or later she's going to find out— even if she never meets your mother. You don't need your mother to embarrass you, Benny Boy. Sooner or later you'll do that all by yourself.*

Ben shook his head the way a dog shakes off water, but he couldn't silence the voice: *This whole situation is hopeless, you know. All you're doing is prolonging the inevitable. You're going to get busted, busted, busted.*

Then Bernie smiled at him and he found himself answering back.

I don't care what you say! he retorted. *I'd be an idiot not to try!*

"Good session!" Dan said, wiping his paint-smudged hands on a rag. Sun streamed through the studio windows behind him, highlighting the curly hair on his arms. "I thought this would be a practice canvas, but the way it's filling up, you may actually have something when you're finished."

"Thanks," Melanie murmured, glad the lesson was over. She'd been shy with her art teacher all afternoon, and he seemed uncomfortable too. Neither of them had mentioned the romantic tension between them on Wednesday, but Melanie hadn't forgotten it.

She was pretty sure Dan hadn't forgotten it either.

"That brushwork is coming along," he said. "Next

Sunday, when I come back, we'll start some knife techniques."

"Okay."

Dan picked up his backpack. Instead of slinging it over his shoulders, though, he stood fooling with its straps. Melanie set down her brush and began wiping her own hands, her eyes finally meeting his.

"This is awkward," he said.

"What is?" But she knew.

"You're awfully young, for one thing. And you're my student on top of that. But I'd really like to see you sometime. Away from here, I mean."

She should have added the fact that she had a boyfriend to Dan's objections. But she didn't.

"You mean like . . . *see* me?" she bleated, taken by surprise. She had prepared herself for more flirting, but she had never expected Dan to be so bold. Especially not with her father right downstairs.

"You don't want to," he said quickly. "Oh, man, I feel like such an idiot."

"Don't." She put a hand on his arm, trying to take away the sting.

"I never should have said anything. I just felt like . . . there seemed to be something . . ." He shook his head, a pink tinge to his tan cheeks. "This is so embarrassing. I imagined the whole thing, right?"

"No," she admitted reluctantly. "You didn't. There *was* something. I'm just not—"

"You're not ready," he interjected, a relieved grin on his handsome face. "It's too soon. I understand."

He didn't. Not exactly. But Melanie didn't correct him as he shrugged into his backpack.

"No need to rush," he added. "I'll see you next Sunday."

Dan winked as he slipped out the studio door. Melanie heard him jump off the bottom stair and land in the entryway before her own feet unfroze from the floor.

"I should have said something!" she moaned to herself. "I should have set him straight."

She didn't know why she hadn't. If Dan had been a high school boy, she'd have put him right in his place.

But he wasn't. He *definitely* wasn't.

So what? The fact that he's totally hot doesn't make things any better.

It made them worse, actually. She couldn't deny she was flattered that a guy like Dan would notice her.

He could have his pick of college girls.

And, after all, he was still her art teacher. She didn't want to offend him—not when she was going to be seeing him every week. It would be too weird to have him come to her house, teaching her to paint, if he was mad at her.

Maybe we could just kind of hang out, she thought. *Go places together as friends.*

The little thrill that idea gave her made her wonder if hanging out with Dan was such a good idea.

Still . . . I'm already in this far. What else am I going to do?

"You're here!" Leah said, opening her front door for Miguel. "Finally."

"I'm not late," Miguel protested, glancing at his watch.

"That wasn't what I meant."

Leah checked the condo hallway to see if any of her neighbors were watching, then quickly pulled him inside. An entire week had already slipped by, and this was the first time he'd come over.

"It's a little dark in here, isn't it?" he asked, squinting around the candlelit living room.

"It's *romantic*," she corrected, towing him to the sofa. She had spent an hour arranging candles all over the condominium, saving the majority of her effort for the coffee table in front of the sofa, where an assortment of low glowing votives surrounded a bowl of floating gardenias. The flowers smelled so good that Leah hadn't been able to resist liberating them from the building's landscaping, and now they perfumed the whole condo. She took a deep breath, wondering if after tonight their scent would always remind her of Miguel, and of what was about to happen between them. . . .

"My sunburn doesn't hurt anymore," she told him, climbing into his lap. She was wearing the backless dress she had planned to wear to the party, its laces crisscrossing skin that had turned brown over the past two days. Miguel ran his hand up under the strings, sending a shiver straight through her.

"So what do you have in mind here?" he asked, his voice dropping huskily.

"I think you know," she whispered back.

Her arms went around him, her hands roving into his dark hair before she moved her lips to his. He fell back into the sofa cushions, a groan rising from his chest as she took her kiss deeper. His arms tightened around her. He pressed the length of his body against hers.

Then he stopped.

"This is really what you want? You're sure?" He was panting, his words forced out between gasps.

"Yes." She had thought about nothing else for days, and she had made her decision.

"I still think we should wait, but I'm only human, Leah."

"This is right," she insisted. "It's time."

"We're not on a schedule." One last hint of doubt lurked in his brown eyes, but his body stayed tight against hers.

"You know what I mean." Her lips found his again, wanting to silence him before he could say more . . . before he could think . . . before he could change her mind. . . .

This is right, she told herself. *It has to be. I love him so much. And I know that he loves me.*

Her hands ran down his back, up his arms, and traveled around to his chest. They were both breathing hard now, focused on the feel of lips, of skin. Leah tried to put everything out of her thoughts but Miguel. She wanted to remember this night all her life. She wanted every detail sharp.

We came so close to never getting here.

She and Miguel had broken up, gotten back together, been engaged, called it off, and had their share of fights. She'd been so discouraged by his lack of interest in her during graduation that she'd nearly gotten involved with a college student named Shane Garrett.

But I never loved Shane, she thought quickly. Sure, he was handsome, and smart, and they had a ton in common. But that wasn't enough. *The entire Shane situation never would have happened if Miguel had just spent a little more time with me. Or if Shane hadn't made himself so totally, completely available . . .*

She moved her hands back into Miguel's hair, annoyed by the way her thoughts were wandering.

Why am I thinking about Shane anyway? I don't miss him, that's for sure. Ever since she and Miguel had hooked him up with Sabrina Ambrosi, Shane had barely even crossed her mind. *I wish he wasn't go-*

ing to Stanford, though. Not that I'm likely to run into him. Much.

"Shane's going to be at Stanford," Leah blurted out. She clapped a hand over her mouth the next instant, unable to believe she had said that aloud, but it was already too late.

"What?" Miguel pushed her off him hard. "You and Shane *again?*"

"No! *Not* me and Shane. And not again. Not ever!"

Miguel was sitting up, his eyes snapping with fury. "He's following you to Stanford?"

"No, he's not *following* me. He was going when I met him. He's been going all along."

"And you're just telling me *now?* What's the *matter* with you?"

Leah was wondering the same thing. She had known she'd have to tell Miguel about Shane's move to California eventually, but she'd been waiting for just the right moment to break the bad news.

And you thought this was it? Any other time would have been better!

"Miguel, don't be mad," she begged.

"Don't be mad?" he said incredulously, surging to his feet. "What am I supposed to be, Leah? Happy? I can't believe you!"

"Where are you going?" she asked, trailing him to the door.

127

"Where do you think I'm going? I'm going home!"

She reached out a hand to stop him, but he was already in the hall.

"Or maybe I'll give Sabrina a call," he shouted before he slammed the front door. "I'm pretty sure *she's* staying in Clearwater Crossing!"

Ten

"We're here!" Peter yelled, opening his front door after camp on Monday. "Come on, Jason. Let's go wash up in the bathroom, and then we'll help my mom make cookies."

"Cookies?" Jason's light blue eyes widened with interest. "What kind of cookies?"

"Whatever kind you want, buddy."

They started walking. "Your house is big," Jason said, following Peter down the hallway.

"You think?" It didn't seem particularly big to Peter. One floor, three bedrooms, two baths, a den . . . pretty standard, really. "It's probably more long than big."

"It seems pretty big to me," Jason said stubbornly.

In the bathroom, Peter turned on the faucet for Jason. "Use soap on those hands," he instructed, grabbing for a washcloth and stuffing it under the stream. "And make sure it gets under those fingernails. Somebody needs to cut those for you."

Jason rolled his eyes, clearly unconcerned. Peter took advantage of the distraction to apply the wet washcloth to Jason's face. The boy was as dirty as always, with a particular concentration of dust clinging to the sticky remnants of a fruit roll around his mouth.

"Hey!" he complained, trying to squirm away.

"Hey, yourself. You're not helping anyone bake looking like that. You don't want to be arrested by the health department, do you?"

"Yeah, right," Jason said, submitting to the washcloth with another roll of his eyes.

Peter knew kids who would have believed that bit about the health department, but Jason wasn't one of them. Foster kids always seemed to see through everything faster somehow. Or maybe they just didn't trust anyone. Not really.

"There you are!" Mrs. Altmann exclaimed when Peter and Jason finally appeared in the kitchen. She had cookie sheets spread out on the counter, and the big electric mixer stood ready for use.

"Hi, Mrs. Altmann," Jason murmured, inexplicably shy all of a sudden. The two had met at Junior Explorers events, most notably on the trip during which Jason had wandered off in a snowstorm and made half the town come look for him. He kept his eyes lowered as he climbed onto a bar stool, getting a bird's-eye view of the cookie action.

"So what are we making today?" she asked. "Chocolate chip? Oatmeal? Peanut butter?"

"Chocolate chip," Jason said quickly, daring to look up. "They're the best."

"They are, aren't they?" Mrs. Altmann agreed with a smile. "There's something about melting chocolate that's pretty hard to beat."

She pulled ingredients out of the refrigerator, then turned to Jason again. "But how will you help me mix them if you're sitting way over there?"

Jason scrambled down from his stool, proudly dumping the things Mrs. Altmann handed him into the mixing bowl and turning the big beater on and off. Peter leaned against the counter watching, a hundred disjointed thoughts in his mind. His mom looked like an old-fashioned stereotype in her apron, her silvering blond hair swept up on top of her head. Jason was Anykid U.S.A. All three of them were smiling as if they didn't have a care in the world. . . .

Looks were so deceiving.

"I can't believe David's missing this," Jason said, greedily licking the beater while Mrs. Altmann put the first sheet of cookies in the oven. "And all for a stupid girl!"

"Hey!" Peter protested. "That 'stupid' girl is Jenna's sister."

Mrs. Altmann chuckled. "David's *marrying* that girl."

A shudder racked Jason's body. "Ick."

While the cookies were baking, Peter dug an old

game of Parcheesi out of the hall closet, and they all sat down to play. Jason demanded the green pieces, which made Peter and his mother both smile— green was the color Peter had always wanted.

"You're pretty good at this, Jason," Mrs. Altmann said as the little boy slammed his pieces around the board, totally absorbed in winning. When he didn't, he immediately insisted on a rematch.

"I was just learning last time," he said, a pleading look on his freckled face.

They were on their second game, and the last sheet of cookies had just come out of the oven, when Mr. Altmann arrived home from work.

"Hey there, Jason," he said pleasantly, setting his briefcase against the wall. "Who's winning?"

"I am," Jason declared intently.

The Altmanns had a long tradition of never "letting" each other win, but when Peter locked eyes with his mother over the game board, he knew they were going to break it. Just this once.

Mr. Altmann took a soda from the refrigerator and pulled up a chair, watching the last few minutes of the game.

"I win!" Jason declared, throwing both fists into the air. "I'm the champion!"

"Okay, champion," Peter's mother teased. "How about helping Peter get these pieces picked up while I put dinner on the table?"

Peter hustled to get the game put away and the

table set while his father went to wash up. Mrs. Alt-mann took a casserole out of her second oven and a bowl of salad from the refrigerator. A few minutes later grace had been said and they were all preparing to eat.

"What is that?" Jason asked suspiciously as Mrs. Altmann served up his plate.

"Chicken noodle casserole."

"It looks funny."

"Well, just give it a try. If you don't like it, you don't have to eat it."

"You're going to like it," Peter assured him, having specifically requested the meal. "It was my favorite when I was your age."

Jason poked at a gravy-coated noodle as if it might be poison, but when he finally tasted it, his eyes went wide.

"Good!" he declared with a full mouth.

Peter's parents exchanged amused glances and passed the bread around.

They talked mostly about camp during dinner, with emphasis on the impending overnight. Jason bragged about the flashlight he'd be bringing as if there had never been any drama about his attending in the first place.

"I'm going to help Peter with something special, too," he announced, reminding Peter that he still needed to think of a suitable job.

For dessert they ate freshly baked cookies, and

since Jason was a guest, Mrs. Altmann let him have as many as he wanted. The boy took advantage of the opportunity by stuffing himself, plugging away at cookie after cookie long after everyone else had finished. Peter gradually began paying more attention to his watch, realizing it was time to get his charge back to Mrs. Brown.

"I'm done," Jason said at last, dropping his half-eaten final cookie. A streak of chocolate smudged one cheek, and his lips were similarly coated.

"Wipe your face, then, because we need to go," Peter told him. "We're already a little late."

Jason took a halfhearted swipe with his napkin and reluctantly rose from the table. "Thanks for the cookies," he said to Mrs. Altmann.

"You're welcome," she told him, beaming at the fact that he hadn't been prompted.

"Come back anytime," Mr. Altmann added.

Jason nodded silently, all the spunk suddenly gone from his step. He trailed Peter, hangdog, to the door, but it wasn't until he was buckled into the car seat that he finally started crying.

"What's the matter, Jason?" Peter asked, turning the engine back off. "I thought we had a good time."

"We did," Jason whimpered, hiding his face in his hands.

"Then what's the matter?"

"Nothing. I . . . just don't want to go back."

"But Mrs. Brown will be worried. She likes you,

you know. She cares about you. If her husband were still alive . . ."

Jason hunched his shoulders up to his ears, sinking into his sobs.

"Come on, buddy," Peter said, rubbing the boy's arm. "Try not to be so upset. I'm going to see you again tomorrow, and in a couple more days we'll all be on the overnight together. Okay?"

Jason managed a nod. Then, lifting the front of his T-shirt to his face, he mopped up his own tears.

"Don't tell anyone about this," he begged, when he could control his voice again. "I know it's stupid. I feel like such a baby."

"You're not a baby," Peter said. "And your secrets are always safe with me."

The wet smile Jason gave him made Peter feel like he'd finally accomplished something.

"What?" Jenna whispered, stunned. "What is this?"

She'd been rooting through the closet she shared with Caitlin, looking for the dress shoes she'd worn to the prom, but she had obviously stumbled across the wrong shoe box. Inside were not the shoes she had wanted but a mess of bridal magazine clippings. For a moment she thought that somehow the ones she'd been cutting had gotten shoved into a box, but a second look revealed that wasn't the case. Jenna's clippings were cut out with scissors, trimmed neatly, and perfectly squared. Half the stuff in the shoe box had been torn haphazardly from the page, and the larger clippings were folded. Jenna *never* folded.

And what is this cake? she asked herself, lifting the top picture for a closer look. *Pink icing? For a wedding cake?*

There was no way she'd saved that one. She didn't even like it.

I don't get it. Is Caitlin keeping a wedding file too? How come I've never seen her work on it?

The answer hit her like a bucketful of cold water. *She is planning things behind my back!*

Caitlin was still out with David that Monday night, so Jenna couldn't confront her directly. Instead she thundered down the two flights of stairs to the ground floor, finding her mother writing a grocery list in the kitchen.

"Look at this!" Jenna said, shoving the open shoe box forward. "I just found this in our closet!"

Mrs. Conrad glanced at the clippings, raised her eyebrows as if failing to see the significance, then added tomatoes to her list.

"Mom! These aren't mine!" Jenna said. "Caitlin must have cut these out herself."

"She *is* the bride," Mrs. Conrad said dryly.

"But—but—*look* at this!" Jenna sputtered, forcing the pink cake picture under her mother's nose. "I've been trying to get Caitlin to order the cake all week and she keeps saying there's no hurry. And now

I find . . . this." Jenna shuddered with distaste. "I think she's planning to order the cake without me!"

Mrs. Conrad pushed her grocery list aside and gave Jenna her full attention. "If she did, would that be a problem?"

"She did?" Jenna cried, devastated. "How *could* she? After everything I've done for her!"

"I didn't say she did," her mother corrected, motioning for Jenna to sit down. "So far as I know, she hasn't. But if she decides she wants to . . ."

"Why would she do that?" Jenna demanded. "I just don't get her, Mom. I'm trying so hard, and I have all these great ideas, and Caitlin barely listens! Every time I want to talk to her about the wedding, it's like she can't run off with David fast enough."

"She *is* marrying him."

"Exactly! She'll have plenty of time to see David later."

Mrs. Conrad shook her head, a slight smile on her face. "You have to give Caitlin a break, Jenna. Maybe if you tried talking to her less, she'd listen to you more."

Jenna didn't like the sound of that. "What do you mean?" she asked suspiciously.

"All I'm saying is, you've been a bit, uh . . . *forceful* with your opinions about the wedding. You know Caitlin would never ask you to stop it, so perhaps she is avoiding you a little."

"What?"

"Just push a little less and—"

"I am not *pushing*!" Jenna interrupted indignantly. "I'm *helping*! If you can't give your own sister wedding advice, who can you give it to?"

"Fine. You asked what I think and now you know."

Mrs. Conrad returned to her shopping list as if Jenna weren't still sitting right in front of her, a picture of a pink cake trembling in her hand. Jenna hesitated a moment, then got to her feet in a huff, hurrying back to her room.

Mom doesn't know what she's talking about. When Caitlin gets home tonight, I'll just ask her!

Nicole slipped into the sewing room and flipped on the overhead light, free at last. Nobody knew she was in there, and no one was likely to find her. Heather had a friend sleeping over, and her parents were watching a movie downstairs. In the sewing room with the door shut behind her, Nicole was finally—blissfully—alone.

What a horrible day, she thought, hiking up her low-hanging overalls to squat beside the cans of paint arranged against one wall.

Since they didn't know what sex the baby was going to be, Mrs. Brewster had decided to go with a neutral, if fairly complicated, paint scheme. The ceiling of the room was white, the walls sage green, and the wooden door and window frame a deeper evergreen. They had put double coats on the walls and ceiling over the weekend. Now Nicole pried the lid off the can of dark green paint and began applying a second coat to the door frame.

I don't even know why I'm doing this, she thought, painting carefully to avoid messing up the adjacent wall. *Mom doesn't know I'm in here, so it's not like I'm getting credit.*

She just didn't feel like being in her own room that night, and she didn't feel much like being anywhere else, either.

Camp that Monday hadn't been particularly bad. She'd shared a group with Melanie and they'd talked mostly about cheerleading. But after that, she'd met Courtney and Gail for a pizza, and they'd given her endless grief.

"Order a *large* pizza, Nicole," Courtney had advised. "You could fit the whole box in those pants and no one would ever notice."

"Very funny." She hadn't told them that the overalls were her new favorite item of clothing, that except for one trip through the laundry she'd been wearing them nonstop since she'd bought them.

"Those pants are obviously comfortable, Courtney," Gail had said, as if to take Nicole's side. "Mind if I climb in there with you, cuz? It looks like there's plenty of room."

Courtney had snorted Sprite through her nose at such a witty remark.

I don't even know why I hang out with those two, Nicole thought, finishing the door frame and setting the paintbrush down on the wet side of the green lid. *All they do is pick on me. Like I wasn't their friend first!*

She felt betrayed, but she would never admit that to either one of them. Courtney was totally back to her old self, and Gail was showing a talent for sarcasm that Courtney could only dream of. They'd eat her alive if she handed them material like that.

Nicole rocked back on her heels and considered a few additional small cans of paint: metallic gold, brown, and a rich deep red. Her mother had jabbered vaguely about murals and stencils when she bought them, but had later admitted she had no plan. Nicole gave the gold a good shake, cracked open the lid, and sat thinking about the color. Cutting some nearby sponges into several different five-pointed stars, she began stamping a constellation on the ceiling, swirling out toward the walls from a center point near the overhead light.

That looks surprisingly good, she decided, wondering if there would be enough paint left over to do the ceiling in her room too. There was something kind of soothing about slapping the stars up overhead, watching the pattern develop. When some gold splattered back down on her overalls she didn't even try to wipe it off. *Stardust*, she thought with a smile.

Then she remembered the worst part of her day, running into Noel as she was leaving the pizza parlor, and her smile shut off like a light. At least he hadn't been with another girl—that would have been devastating. He had been there with guy friends and she had been there with girl friends; everything should have been all right. But Nicole couldn't stop worrying about it. If Courtney and Gail had given her a hard time about her outfit, Noel had bested them easily. The appalled curl of his lip had spoken louder than words ever could.

"I, uh, I just got off camp," Nicole had offered by way of excuse, glad that at least the tube top she was wearing under her overall bib revealed glimpses of skin at her sides. Noel liked her to dress sexy—especially when his friends were around.

"So I see." His eyes had dropped her quickly, skipping into the crowded restaurant.

"Maybe we can do something this weekend," she'd said, sounding totally desperate. "I have an overnight on Thursday, but I'll be back Friday evening."

He had nodded slightly—whether to agree or simply show that he'd heard her, Nicole hadn't been sure.

"I'll call you," he'd said vaguely, leading his friends off toward a table without waiting for the hostess. The pair of them had smirked at her as they'd gone by, making her feel even worse.

On the drive home, Courtney and Gail had laughed about Nicole's terrible timing, offering to burn the offending overalls to save her from future faux pas. Thinking about it now, Nicole could barely hold back the tears.

How shallow can people be? They only like me when I'm skinny and made up and dressed to their specifications? Who needs them, anyway?

She pressed out a few more stars, then abruptly sat down in the middle of the floor and cried.

I do, she thought miserably.

Eleven

"Is something the matter, Leah?" asked Nicole.

Their camp groups were eating lunch together on the benches, giving the older girls a chance to talk, but so far there hadn't been much conversation. They'd been quiet for so long, in fact, that the question took Leah by surprise.

"No," she said quickly. "I mean . . ." She didn't want to explain, so in the end she shrugged. "I'm just not having the best week, that's all."

"Tell me about it!" Nicole exclaimed, rolling her eyes.

Leah wondered if she was supposed to ask what Nicole's problem was, but she didn't. She had problems enough of her own.

If he would just look at me, Leah thought, straining to catch Miguel's eye. But he and Jesse were sitting with their group all the way down at the dock—a location she couldn't help believing was no coincidence since everyone usually ate on the benches.

At least I'm pretty sure he's not blabbing to Jesse about what happened.

143

Talking was not Miguel's favorite thing in general, and a person needed a crowbar to pry anything personal out of him. Still . . . the fact that he didn't want to talk to *her* hurt so much she could barely stand it. They hadn't spoken since he'd stormed out of her house Sunday night, raving about hooking up with Sabrina.

Not that I think he actually called her, Leah reassured herself quickly. *We're going to make up*.

But on Monday Miguel had worked at the hospital instead of coming to camp, and so far that Tuesday he'd done everything possible to avoid eye contact, obviously still furious about Shane's attending Stanford.

Like I have any control over that, she thought, trying to lean more into his line of sight. *My only mistake was telling him*.

Especially right then.

"I'm, uh . . . I'm going to the outhouse," Leah told Nicole. "Can you keep an eye on my group for a few minutes?"

Nicole nodded and Leah made her escape. She didn't really need to use the outhouse—nothing on Earth could have made her step into one of those stinky, fly-filled plastic cubes—but she did need a few minutes to herself. Sliding off the edge of the split-log bench, Leah wandered slowly across the clearing in the direction of the outhouses, her eyes glued to the back of Miguel's head.

It just didn't seem possible, everything that had gone wrong in her life in the past few days. Instead of the romantic two weeks she had expected when her parents left, first she had gotten poison ivy, then a sunburn, then the inexplicably self-destructive urge to blurt out something she had known and been hiding for weeks. . . .

It's almost like I don't want *anything to happen with Miguel.*

The thought stopped her dead in the middle of the clearing. Could that be the answer?

After all, I know what poison ivy looks like. I knew what I was wading into, but I went after that ball anyway. And then the sunburn . . . of course I was going to get burned wearing that top all day. And as far as telling Miguel about Shane goes, what did I think? That he'd be happy?

She imagined him mentioning Sabrina in that same intimate moment . . . then imagined herself killing him. Even the instant she was blurting out Shane's name, she had known how inappropriate it was.

She started walking again, in a hurry now to reach the sheltering trees on the other side of the clearing. As soon as she did, she ducked behind a big one, finding a hidden seat on a rock.

I sabotaged myself! The realization sank slowly into her disbelieving brain. *How could I have done that?*

After all, she was the one who'd decided she

wanted to take things farther in the first place. She was the one who'd insisted, despite Miguel's objections. How could she have been so wrong?

Maybe . . . well . . . I guess I could have confused opportunity with obligation. Just because my parents aren't home doesn't mean I have to do the things I wouldn't if they were here.

It even seemed kind of silly now, the way she had always just assumed that they were the ones holding her back. Because now that they weren't . . .

They never were, she realized. They tell me their expectations, but I decide what I do. And when. And with whom. If Miguel and I had been determined to have sex, my parents wouldn't have needed to leave the state to make it happen. Mom and Dad haven't been stopping me. I've been stopping me.

She'd been stopping herself right up to that very minute. She felt like running to Miguel, throwing her arms around his neck, and explaining the whole epiphany. Everything made so much sense now! She was sure he would understand.

Except that Miguel wasn't speaking to her. After the way she'd just messed up, it could be weeks before he decided he would. And every precious day was one less day of summer, one less day they had together before she moved away.

A hot tear coursed down Leah's cheek.

How could something that was supposed to be so good have turned out so awful?

*   *   *

"Ben! Ben, hi!"

Bernie's voice rang out as the Junior Explorers' bus pulled into the parking lot at Clearwater Crossing Park after camp, making Ben sit up straight. Through his open window he spotted his girlfriend waving from the edge of the pavement with one skinny arm.

"Hi, Bernie!" he called back eagerly. He hadn't expected her to be there, which made her appearance a double thrill. Ever since Sunday, when he'd miraculously pulled off that game of musical chairs between Bernie and his mother, he'd been worried that she suspected something. Or, at the very least, that she thought he was weird.

You are *weird*, he reminded himself. But the bright, happy smile on Bernie's face seemed to say she didn't know that.

"I'm getting off!" Ben blurted out, jumping to his feet. His backpack snagged on the edge of his seat as he did, nearly yanking him back down. He lurched backward, then managed to redirect his momentum, stumbling over Elton's feet on his way into the aisle.

"Let me out first!" he begged, racing toward the front of the bus. If the kids started getting out in front of him, he could be stuck on the bus forever.

"In a hurry to see someone?" David Altmann teased, his hand resting lazily on the metal handle that opened the bus door.

"Ben's got a girlfriend!" some of the nearby campers started chanting.

"Open the door before this gets ugly," Ben begged, and David finally did.

Ben charged down the bus stairs, nearly falling again as he hit the blacktop. One ankle folded beneath him, throwing all his weight to that side. He recovered and slowed down, doing his best not to limp or wince as he made his way to Bernie.

"Hi!" she said again, grinning, clearly glad to see him. It was nothing short of amazing to see a girl look at him that way. Ben wanted to lift her up and swing her around in circles, but instead he played it cool.

"Hi. What are you doing here?" he asked.

"I came to pick up Elton." Her brown eyes sparkled with mischief. "But also to see you."

"Pick up Elton?" Bernie would be a ninth grader in the fall. Driving was still a couple years off.

"My mom had to work a long shift and I was just over at the clinic, so she sent me to get him and walk him home. Not that I minded," she added, grinning. "Especially since I've been entering data all day."

"Yeah?" Ben stretched up a little taller, his body unconsciously mimicking the way she made him feel. He started walking toward the sidewalk. "Come on, I'll walk home with you."

Bernie smiled. "Shouldn't we get Elton first?"

"Huh? Oh! I mean . . . obviously."

He started back toward the bus, hoping to sepa-

148

rate Elton from the usual afternoon muddle, but the boy had spotted his sister and was already headed toward them.

"Come on, Elton! I'm walking you home," Ben called, trying to hurry the boy along. The quicker they all got away from the crowd, the sooner Ben could relax.

"You're walking *me?*" Elton repeated skeptically, as if he'd deduced the real object of Ben's interest.

"Well, yeah. And Bernie's coming with us."

They had cleared the after-camp chaos and were traipsing along Clearwater Boulevard, Elton out in front, before Ben finally dared to breathe; another tricky situation had been handled without any of his so-called friends blowing his cover.

His sense of relief didn't last very long.

"Hey, do you know Maude Pipkin?" Bernie asked abruptly.

Ben almost swallowed his tongue. "Wh-wh-why do you ask?"

"I entered her record today at work, and I figured you must know her. How many Pipkins can there be?"

Bernie had entered his mother's record? That meant she knew how much his mother weighed! *Ben* didn't even know how much his mother weighed. There were certain mysteries best left unsolved.

"Well, I uh . . . I'm sure there must be dozens of Pipkins that I know nothing about."

Bernie gave him a strange look. "Really?"

"Why not?"

"I never heard that name before."

"I never met a brother and sister named for Elton John and Bernie Taupin before, but here you are. Clearwater Crossing is a strange and amazing place."

Bernie giggled. "Strange and amazing?"

"Well. Strange, anyway."

"So then this Maude—"

"What else did you do at work today?" Ben interrupted desperately. "Better still, what are you doing tonight? Do you have anything fun planned?"

"Oh, yeah," Bernie said disbelievingly. "Baby-sitting's always a ton of fun."

Elton twisted around on the sidewalk to make a face at her.

"If I was baby-sitting Elton, I'll bet we *would* have fun," Ben said.

Elton shook his head sadly; Ben had clearly lost favor by taking a liking to his sister. The boy kicked a rock along the edge of the grass, and Ben returned his attention to Bernie.

"You know, I read a great article in *Super Computer* this month," he said. "Do you get that magazine?"

"No!" she said indignantly. "I mean, uh . . . why would I? I'm not, like, a computer *geek* or anything."

"Of course not," Ben said quickly. He knew what computer geeks looked like, and they didn't look like

Bernie. He decided not to mention that he had a subscription to *Super Computer*.

"You know what's weird?" Bernie asked. "Fireflies. Fireflies are weird. I mean, how do they light up?"

"I don't know." Was Bernie changing the subject now? If so, Ben was happy to help her. "I think it's called phosphorescence. Or maybe luminescence."

"Yes, but how does it *work?*"

"We can probably find out on the Internet."

"Computers again?" she said, sounding exasperated. "Is that all you ever think about?"

"No," he said defensively. "No, I also think about . . . ice cream," he improvised, spotting a little shop up ahead. "What do you say we stop for a sundae? My treat."

"Yeah!" Elton shouted, liking him again. "I want a banana split."

"That's too big," said Bernie. "It will spoil your dinner."

"If Mom's not coming home until late, I'll eat it *for* my dinner."

Bernie started to argue, then shrugged. "Why not? That's one less pot of macaroni and cheese I have to make."

Ben opened the ice cream parlor door, relieved to have successfully derailed Bernie's inquiries about his mother. Still, there was no way to tell when she might raise the subject again. He ate his ice cream nervously, barely tasting the double scoop he had ordered.

Would Bernie be more persistent next time?

"What a day!" Peter groaned, dropping his back-pack, wet towel, and bathing suit onto his bedroom floor. The ride home from camp in the bus had been particularly brutal that Tuesday, and he was craving a long, hot shower. But first he needed to call Jenna.

I wish I'd asked her about the groceries while I had the chance. Caitlin had driven to the park to meet the bus, and she, David, Peter, and Jenna had all stood around talking for at least fifteen minutes before David decided to go home with Caitlin—or, more likely, to cruise by the Conrads' just long enough to drop Jenna off. Peter had ended up with a car to him-self and enough time on the ride home to realize he hadn't asked Jenna if they'd have enough donated food for Thursday's overnight. If not, he'd need to make some reminder calls to parents.

He was reaching for his phone, about to pick it up, when a muffled sound made him freeze, listening.

What's that?

The gasping, gurgling noise seemed to be coming through the wall from David's bedroom, but that was impossible. David wasn't home. It stopped abruptly, and Peter was just relaxing his ears when it started up again.

What is *that?* He was never going to be able to concentrate on groceries now, not until he found out.

Out in the hallway, he confirmed that the sound was coming from David's room. His brother's door was pushed shut but not latched, a sliver of light glowing along its edge. Peter tiptoed to the door and slowly pushed it open. Inside, his mother was sitting on David's neatly made bed, crying into her hands.

"Mom! What are you doing?" Peter yelped, filled with dread at the unexpected sight. He ran into the room and dropped to his knees beside her. "What happened? What's wrong? Why are you in here?" He fired off his questions, afraid to give her a chance to answer one. He couldn't remember the last time he'd seen her cry.

His mother had lifted her face and now she dried it with her palms, attempting to smile as if nothing had happened.

"Peter! You're home early."

"No, I'm not. What's going on?"

"I wasn't expecting you yet, that's all."

"So you thought you'd come in David's room and cry about it? Mom, what's the matter? You're scaring me."

She glanced nervously at the open doorway. "Is David home too?"

Peter shook his head. "He went to Caitlin's."

"Your father?"

"Not yet."

"Well, that's a relief, anyway." She took a tissue from her pocket and blew her nose, giving up the attempt to pretend everything was normal. "This is so embarrassing."

"What is?" Peter asked, only slightly reassured. "Why were you crying?"

She smiled sadly and laid one hand against his cheek. "You're too young to understand," she said ruefully. "Lucky you."

"Try me," he insisted.

Mrs. Altmann took a long look around the room before she answered, as if memorizing the contents of David's bulletin board, the pictures on the walls, the trophies on his shelves.

"I guess the idea of David getting married and moving away is finally catching up to me," she said. "Don't misunderstand me—Caitlin's a good girl. I'm sure they'll be very happy. It's just . . . I guess I'm having a hard time letting go. I'm going to miss him so much!"

Peter felt a lump rise in his throat as he took his mother's hands. "Why wouldn't I understand that?" he asked. "I'm going to miss him too. But it won't really be that different from having him in college, will it? We'll probably see him just as much."

She nodded quickly. "You're right. But there was a chance before . . . I mean, he *could* have taken a job in Clearwater Crossing. I always kind of hoped he'd come back here after college."

"To live at home? Isn't he kind of old for that?"

"No, not in the *house*, but . . ." She sighed, her shoulders dropping as she exhaled. "You're right. I'm being silly."

"It's not silly, Mom."

"Yes. It is." She took one last swipe at her tears, then fixed Peter with pleading eyes. "Don't tell anyone about this," she begged. "I know it's stupid. I just feel like I'm losing my baby."

Twelve

"I just don't feel like going," Nicole told Courtney on the phone Wednesday night. "I don't even know why you're asking me, now that you have Gail."

"I don't *have* Gail—I *know* Gail. You're still my best friend, Nicole."

It didn't feel that way, but Nicole was too upset to discuss the weird triangle that she, Courtney, and Gail had somehow become. If she tried to tell Court how she felt, she'd only end up crying—and then she'd feel even worse.

"Just, go have fun at the movies, all right? I'll see you Friday when I get back from the overnight."

"I thought you were going out with Noel on Friday."

"Oh. Right."

How could she have forgotten something so important? Maybe because, far from looking forward to them, Nicole was starting to dread her encounters with Noel.

"I'll see you Saturday, then," she told Courtney,

hanging up the phone. She stared down at the receiver a moment, wondering if she'd made the right decision, then hitched her overalls up by the straps and walked the short distance from her room to the baby's. Shutting the door behind her again, she did a slow, satisfied turn, admiring her handiwork.

All the woodwork had two coats of glossy dark green paint now, and the ceiling sparkled with gold stars. Best of all, Nicole had used some of the leftover evergreen paint to freehand a vine climbing alongside and over the doorway. Brown stems and tiny red berries made the foliage look like something from a fairy-tale forest, especially with the stars. There really wasn't anything left to paint, but the cans were still in the room, and after a minute Nicole decided to try her hand at a matching swag of greenery over the square window.

It looks too plain with just those shutters.

She had barely begun with the brown, carefully painting the stems she would later fill with leaves, when her mother came in without knocking.

"Nicole!" she said cheerfully. "I thought I heard you rooting around in here. What are you doing now?"

The question sounded innocent, but Nicole turned slowly from the window, prepared for anything. She hadn't asked her mother when she'd made her other decorating modifications either, and so far Mrs.

Brewster had taken them in stride, but everyone had a limit. Nicole knew from experience that her mother often reached hers all at once.

"I just thought . . . ," she said meekly, "I mean, this window looks kind of plain now. . . ."

"Are you painting another vine like the one by the door? That came out really well."

"Yeah. I thought so too," Nicole replied, daring to breathe again.

Her mother stood in the center of the room, both hands resting on her belly, and eventually Nicole turned her back and started painting again.

"You know . . . ," her mother said tentatively behind her. "I really appreciate everything you're doing to help fix up this room, Nicole. For a while you had me thinking that you'd never accept this baby. I can't tell you how relieved I am to see you finally coming around."

Nicole kept her eyes on her painting. Was that what her mother thought? That she was "coming around" to the idea of the baby?

Just because painting turned out to be kind of fun, and I've ended up spending kind of a lot of time in here, doesn't mean I want that baby. She wasn't sure what it meant, actually, but it didn't have to mean *that*.

Nicole heard the door shut behind her and turned to see if her mom had gone, but Mrs. Brewster was walking back toward her, a conspirator's grin on her face.

"If I tell you a secret," she whispered, "do you *promise* not to tell your father or Heather?"

Nicole's heart beat a bit faster. She'd never been able to pass up an opportunity to know something Heather didn't. "All right."

Her mother smiled excitedly. "When I went to the doctor yesterday . . . I kind of glanced at the sonogram at the wrong time. And I saw . . . well . . . let's just say it seemed pretty obvious, so I went ahead and confirmed it with the doctor. Are you ready?"

Nicole nodded, the suspense killing her.

"You're going to have a brother!" her mom announced.

"You're kidding!" Nicole squealed, forgetting to be quiet. This was big news. Huge! She couldn't believe her mother was telling it to her before anyone else. "You're really not going to tell Dad?"

"He wants to be surprised."

"I *know*, but . . . wow!"

Mrs. Brewster chuckled and put a cautionary finger to her lips. "If you don't keep your voice down, you're going to tell him yourself."

"Oh! Right," Nicole whispered, cringing. "But Mom! This is . . ." She shook her head, at a loss for words. "This is . . . great," she managed at last.

"Yeah?" her mom said. "Really?"

Her expression was so hopeful that in that instant Nicole finally understood how much her selfish behavior had hurt her. She had wanted her mother to feel the same pain the baby had caused her, and she had obviously succeeded. The thing was, she just didn't hurt like she had anymore. At least, not about the baby.

"Really," Nicole said. "I'm glad."

And then she surprised them both by reaching around Mrs. Brewster's midsection, giving her mom and new brother both a hug.

"You did *what?*" Jenna exclaimed, sitting up in bed so fast she scattered her magazines. "I thought you *liked* the veil!"

Caitlin shrugged as she walked to their bedroom closet and hung up her white sweater, back from another date with David. "I really wanted a hat all along."

"Yes, but we *agreed* on the veil," Jenna insisted, unable to believe her ears. "You just went back and exchanged it? Without even asking me?"

"I didn't know I had to." Caitlin peeled her dress off over her head and began changing into her pajamas, keeping her back to Jenna.

"Well, no. I'm not saying you *had* to." Jenna sighed as she tried to reimagine the wedding party with Caitlin wearing a hat. "What does the hat look like?"

"It's small. Simple. Plain."

Surprise, Jenna thought, doing her best to hide how disappointed she was. *Everything Caitlin picks is plain.*

She had so wanted her sister to have a fairy-tale wedding, but how could they when everything Caitlin picked was small? And simple.

And plain.

"Well, maybe we can decorate it with flowers," Jenna said. "I have a whole bunch of clippings for flower ideas, but I haven't had a chance to put them in my book yet. I'll just get my folder and—"

"Thanks, but that's okay," Caitlin said, crossing the room and dropping onto her bed. "I ordered the flowers this afternoon."

"You *what?*"

Caitlin shrugged again. "I was in the neighborhood, so I figured I might as well."

"But Caitlin!" It was bad enough that Jenna hadn't had an opportunity to compile her photographs yet; Caitlin hadn't even looked at them! Jenna hadn't had the chance to advise her sister on floral themes or motifs or color combinations. They hadn't discussed altar arrangements, or whether to have pew bows. They hadn't discussed anything! "I can't believe you didn't take me with you."

"You were at camp."

"Yes, but if I'd known you were going to order the flowers, I would have taken today off."

"That would have been a waste of your time. I wasn't there an hour."

"But Caitlin . . . ," Jenna whined. Did her sister honestly believe she had done her a favor? After all the work Jenna had put into the wedding? "I wanted to help you."

"Help me do what?"

"Help you choose!"

"Oh. Thanks, but I already knew what I wanted."

"What?" Jenna asked. "What did you order?"

"Daisies, mostly."

"Daisies!" Jenna exclaimed, overwhelmed with disappointment. "*Daisies?* Are you kidding me?"

Caitlin drew back on her bed, her brown eyes widening. "I like daisies."

"I know you *like* them, Cat, but this is a *wedding*. You want long-stemmed roses, or orchids, or tulips, or something *special*—not some weed we could cut in our own backyard."

"Daisies are not weeds," Caitlin said in a low voice.

"Close enough. Listen," Jenna said desperately, "there's still time to change your order. Right? This weekend, when I get back from the overnight, we can go through all my ideas and—"

"I don't want to change my order."

"But you *will*!" Jenna insisted. "I have such great ideas. If you would just let me show you what I want to—"

"Why is what you want more important than what I want?"

There was an edge to Caitlin's voice that Jenna hadn't heard before. Her shy sister almost never interrupted people either. But Jenna was so upset about

162

being left out of the hat and flower decisions that she forged ahead anyway.

"It's not *more* important. It's—"

"It's not even *as* important," Caitlin said.

"Well—but—I thought we were working as a team!" Jenna sputtered, taken aback.

"I never said that. You just started taking over."

"Taking *over*? No way! Just because I want everything to be perfect for you doesn't—"

"You want everything to be perfect for *you*," Caitlin snapped in a tone Jenna had definitely never heard before. "Well, I'm sorry, but I've got news for you, Jenna. You're not the one getting married!"

Jenna was stunned. She opened her mouth but couldn't think of a reply. Caitlin reached over and flipped out the light on the nightstand. Jenna heard her flop back into the blankets, leaving Jenna sitting alone in the darkness.

"I never said—" she began.

"You've argued with every decision I've made. You hated the dresses, the colors, the shoes, the hats, and now the flowers. I'm done letting you make me feel bad about my own wedding, Jenna. I'm just not going to talk to you about it anymore."

Jenna could feel her jaw working up and down long before any words came out. "But Caitlin! That's—"

"I'm not talking about it! Good night."

Jenna heard her sister turn her back, signifying the end of the conversation.

I can't believe her! Jenna thought, sinking slowly into her own blankets. She was shocked that Caitlin could accuse her of trying to take over. And, the more she thought about it, she was pretty offended, too.

I've been busting my hump on this wedding while she's been running around with David, not a care in the world. All I wanted was to help her, so that she'd have something nice.

Jenna pulled the covers up over her head, hiding from the injustice. *And if I've been a little opinionated— if I have—it was only for Caitlin's own good. Look what she picked on her own! She'd be a lot better off if she'd listened to me!*

An angry tear ran down Jenna's cheek and disappeared into her pillow. It hurt to be accused of having ulterior motives when she didn't.

That's the thanks I get for trying to help! she thought, flopping over to turn her back on Caitlin. *Well, I'm not helping anymore. Caitlin can ruin things all by herself!*

I just don't see how this can turn out good, Ben worried, tossing in his sweaty sheets. *I'm in way over my head.*

So far he had managed to prevent Bernie from learning anything too personal about him, but he couldn't keep that up forever. The way things were heading lately, he'd be surprised if he could keep it up another week.

I never should have tried to trick her in the first place, he thought unhappily. *If I hadn't tried to pretend I was something I wasn't, I wouldn't be in this mess now.*

He rolled over to check his alarm clock, groaning at what he saw. It was nearly midnight, and he was supposed to leave on the overnight with the Junior Explorers in the morning. He needed to get his sleep now, because he could forget about resting during the next two days.

It's not like I tried to trick her, he justified himself. *Not much, anyway. She already thought I was cool when she met me, from listening to Elton. Isn't it kind of her own fault, for taking a seven-year-old's opinion?*

Ben rolled over again, tangling a blanket around his neck.

She's going to find out. I'm having to make up stories every time I see her, and that's just not right.

He didn't want to lie to Bernie. He *liked* Bernie. Sometimes, when he let himself, he even thought he might love her.

I have to break up with her.

It was the only solution.

At least if I break up with her now, before she learns what I'm really like, she might be sorry to see me go.

The other alternative was to wait for *her* to break up with *him*, to see the disgust in her eyes when she realized what a loser he really was.

Ben shuddered at the thought. If it was over, he at least wanted to walk away with some pride. He wanted to remember the way Bernie's eyes had lit up when she saw him, and the perfect way she had smiled at him when they met. To see those same lips sneer would break his heart.

So that's it, then, he concluded. *I'll tell her as soon as I get back from the overnight. The sooner the better, in fact.*

Because he knew if he waited much longer, he'd never be able to do it.

Thirteen

"Peter!" Jason cried, running up with a tragic expression on his face. "Peter, the batteries in my flashlight are dead!"

"Already? It's not even dark yet."

It felt as if they had barely finished setting up camp. The bus had been at least an hour late leaving the parking lot after all the sleeping bags, extra equipment, and groceries had been packed. The wood for the bonfire alone had taken a ridiculous amount of time to stow under the seats, and then had slid out into the aisle every time David hit a bump. Luckily Mr. Altmann, Chris Hobart, and a couple of the kids' parents had been along to take care of keeping the walkways clear.

"I think it came on in my duffel," Jason said.

"*Came* on? Or got *left* on after you were done showing off in the parking lot?"

Jason shrugged. "I need new batteries."

"Do you see a store out here?" Peter asked, gesturing around them. The primitive site they'd hiked to was a small clearing smack up against a gravelly cove. The firewood had been stacked in the center of the open space, and backpacks, sleeping bags, and tarps took up every level inch around that. The groceries were stashed in coolers and crates under the trees at one edge, as far from the pit toilet as possible. "Where am I supposed to get batteries, Jason?"

"David will have to go back for them in the bus."

Peter couldn't suppress a bark of laughter. "Not going to happen, my friend. Are you kidding me?"

All the adults were exhausted from dragging in so much gear, and most of them, including David, were now sitting in shallow water, keeping an eye on the kids who wanted to swim. The male members of Eight Prime were trying to keep track of the kids playing hide-and-seek in the trees around the edges of the clearing, while the girls were in the middle of making peanut butter sandwiches for everybody.

"Peter!" Jason's voice turned whiny. "I need batteries."

"Why don't you go swimming?" Peter suggested. "Or go see what Jesse is doing."

Jason didn't bite. "You said I was going to help you with something important."

The boy still obviously idolized Jesse, but in the past few days he seemed to be switching at least some of his allegiance back to Peter. Peter took it as a sign that all the extra attention he'd been giving Jason lately was paying off. After all, he and Jason went back a lot farther than Jason and Jesse.

"You are. Tonight," Peter said, relieved he had finally thought of a job. "You're going to help me do the bed check. We'll go all around the camp together and make sure everyone's in their sleeping bags. You'll be the last kid in bed."

"Cool," Jason breathed, his blue eyes full of excitement. Then he remembered his problem. "How am I going to do that without a flashlight?" he moaned. "Peter!"

"You can use mine," Peter said quickly.

"But mine is better!"

"You can have the batteries out of mine, then."

The smile the little boy gave him was worth a much larger sacrifice.

"You know, Jason," Peter said impulsively, "whatever happens, you and I will still be friends. Wherever you end up living, I'll come visit you."

"Really?" Jason seemed reluctant to believe another promise that might be broken.

If they'll let me, Peter thought uneasily, but he didn't say that. They *had* to let him—it would be too cruel if they didn't.

"Really," he promised. "Of course."

Leah dragged another log over to the fire, so mentally focused on Miguel that she barely saw the cross-legged campers she had to weave through, or the other members of Eight Prime. Dinner was over, the mess cleaned up, and Ben was attempting to interest

169

the kids in campfire songs. So far they seemed a lot more interested in the marshmallows Jenna, Melanie, and a couple of the parents were helping them roast on sticks, taking the ones that didn't get completely charred to Jesse and Nicole for assembly into s'mores.

Where did he go? Leah wondered as she dropped her log into the flames, inadvertently causing a shower of sparks that sent the marshmallow roasters scrambling.

"Leah!" several complained. "You're wrecking it!"

"You should be more careful," Amy Robbins informed her solemnly.

"You're right. Sorry." Leah backed away from the roaring fire, figuring she'd done enough damage for the present. Her eyes combed the woods on all sides of the clearing, looking for Miguel.

She'd seen him and Peter not long ago, playing with a few of the boys down by the water. It was getting too dark for fooling around on the shore now, though. *Where could he have gone?*

She kept backing up until she was on the outer edge of the crowd, all the while scanning for a familiar dark head, but Miguel was nowhere to be seen. He'd been ignoring her all day, even on a couple of occasions when he'd had to walk right past her. By now all of Eight Prime had to know they were fighting, although so far no one had said anything.

If he would just listen to me for five minutes, I know I could explain. He has to be as tired of fighting as I am.

Doesn't he?

Making up with Miguel was all she'd been able to think about for days. Not only were they losing precious time together, it killed her to have him mad at her—especially since it was all her fault.

I have to find him and apologize. I can't take this anymore.

She would have apologized long before, if he'd given her even the slightest chance.

"How's it going, Leah?" a friendly voice asked behind her. She turned to see Chris Hobart, Peter's original partner in the Junior Explorers. "Aren't you having a s'more?"

She shrugged. "Maybe later."

"That's exactly what Miguel said," Chris told her with a laugh. "Do you two compare notes or something?"

"Did you just see him? Do you know where he is?" she asked urgently.

Chris pointed back toward the water. "He said something about walking along the shore and finding a better place for the kids to swim tomorrow. The bottom here is pretty rocky."

"He's doing that *now*?" Leah protested. "But it's dark!"

"That's what I said. At least he has a flashlight."

Leah had one too, in her backpack, but she didn't waste time going to get it. She'd been looking for a chance to get Miguel alone for days, and now she finally had one.

"Thanks, Chris," she said, running off in the direction he had pointed.

Her eyes adjusted quickly as she got farther from the fire. Full dark hadn't yet fallen, and there was enough remaining light to see obstacles in the clearing. Under the trees was a different story, though. Leah stayed close to the water, half afraid of what might be waiting to run out from the woods and grab her. Her ankles were wrenched in the loose gravel as she hurried along in search of Miguel, breathing a sigh of relief when she saw the beam of a flashlight raking the dark water up ahead. She forced her way across a brushy little point, then froze, arrested by the beauty of the scene in front of her. Miguel was standing alone in the center of a perfect cove, his feet underlain by a half-moon of pale sand. His flashlight swept slowly across the dark ripples, its beam like bursts of diamonds on the water. At last the light came to rest on her.

"It took you long enough," he said.

"You were waiting for me?"

"I figured you'd show up eventually."

She hurried forward across the sand, ignoring the cool grains overtopping her sneakers and flowing in around her feet. "You didn't make it easy to find you."

He shrugged. "You managed."

She stopped directly in front of him, her heart pounding at the realization that they hadn't been so close to each other in days. And he was talking to her too—at least enough to let her speak her piece.

"I just want to say I'm sorry," she blurted out. "I should have told you about Shane before."

"It sure seems that way to me." He looked past her, out to the water.

"It was just that I knew you were going to get mad, and it doesn't *mean* anything. I wouldn't go out with Shane if he paid me. I never want to see that guy again!"

"But you're going to," Miguel said sullenly. "You're going to see him at Stanford."

"I might run into him," she allowed. "By accident. But a college campus is a big place, and we're studying totally different things. Besides, he'll be a graduate student and I'll be a freshman. There would be practically no reason for us ever—"

"I get the idea," Miguel interrupted. "If it's really no big deal, why did you wait so long to tell me?"

"Because I'm an idiot!" Leah groaned. "I don't know what else to say. I'm really sorry I didn't."

"Okay."

She hesitated, uncertain what he meant. "Okay? Does that mean you forgive me?"

He shrugged again. "I guess."

She threw her arms around him, burying her face

in his warm sweatshirt and inhaling his familiar scent. She had missed him so much!

"I still don't understand why you told me when you did, though," he said, his voice rumbling in her ear. "Talk about killing a mood . . ."

"I know the answer to that now," she admitted. "Things were getting pretty hot, and, well . . . I guess I chickened out."

"It was your idea!" he exclaimed.

"Yes, but . . ." She lifted her head to look into his eyes. "Maybe it wasn't such a good one."

The last trace of sullenness left his face. He clicked off the flashlight and put his arms around her.

"Why didn't you just tell me *that*? I would have agreed with you."

"I know," she admitted, snuggling back into his sweatshirt. "But it took me a while to figure it out."

They stood that way a long time, Leah's head rising and falling with his breathing. Gradually she realized she felt more at peace than she had for a long time, since way before her parents left. A load had been lifted from her, one she hadn't even known she was carrying.

"So, will you come over Saturday night?" she asked at last. "I'll make dinner for us."

He hesitated, then rested his head on hers. "Yes," he whispered. "I'll be there."

* * *

Melanie tossed uneasily in her sleeping bag, half-conscious of what was coming, powerless to stop it.

"No," she murmured in her sleep, but the sound wasn't loud enough to wake her. The dream creeping into her brain seemed to shut off her outside senses.

In Melanie's mind, she was standing beside her mother's open grave, looking down through the moist, crumbling earth into an open casket. Her mother's eyes were closed, her blond hair arranged on a white satin pillow. Melanie knew her mother was dead, but she stood motionless at the top of the hole, unable to believe it.

Maybe she's just asleep, she thought. *They've buried her too soon!*

She needed to get her mother out right away. But instead she stood there, paralyzed. Suddenly the coffin lid snapped shut, closing on its own. A clod of dirt fell into the hole, thudding on the polished white lid.

"No!" Melanie cried. Her body jerked forward and the next thing she knew she was standing in the hole, one foot on each side of the coffin. She grabbed the lid by its edge, bending over the casket and straining to open it, but it seemed to be sealed shut. Then something hit the back of her head.

"Not the dirt," she moaned, aware even in her dream that this had happened before. She lifted her face in time to see the walls of the grave start caving in.

She screamed, but there was no one to hear. Dirt began pouring in, covering her feet, her knees, the lid of the casket. She tried to pull her feet free, but the dirt was falling so fast that she couldn't get on top of it. It was up to her thighs, the coffin was completely covered, and she was trapped.

"Help! Help me!" she screamed, choking on the soil raining down all around her. "I'm not dead. I'm alive!"

No one came to her rescue. The dirt was up to her waist, then her chest. Melanie screamed again, and again, frantic to get free.

"Help me!" she begged. "I'm not dead!"

The dirt was up to her neck and climbing. Her arms were trapped at her sides; she couldn't dig away the soil beginning to fill her screaming mouth. It covered her nose, then, in one horrible rush, her eyes. Melanie was in darkness, her last bit of air burning in her lungs. She was suffocating. If she didn't get a breath in the next few seconds . . .

She bolted upright in her sleeping bag, still half-asleep as she filled her lungs with air. Then she screamed for all she was worth.

The sound opened her eyes, her heart racing as she jolted into wakefulness. And in the chaos that ensued, Melanie realized she hadn't screamed just in her dream.

"What? What was that?" kids' voices bleated all around her. A few of them started to cry.

"Who screamed?" Peter demanded. "Is everyone okay?"

"I *told* you guys not to tell ghost stories," Jenna's sleepy voice accused from the other side of the fire. The logs had long since burned down to coals, barely glowing now. Flashlights began to flip on, looking for the source of the disturbance. A few of the adults got up and began checking everyone.

Melanie sat shivering in her sleeping bag at the edge of the woods, sweat soaking through her T-shirt. The only thing more terrifying than having that old nightmare again was having it in public. She knew she should confess to the scream and set people's minds at ease, but then she'd have to explain that she'd had a bad dream—and that was far too private. She huddled uncertainly in the darkness, pulling the wadded sleeping bag tight against her chest until gentle arms slipped around her from behind.

"Bad dream?" Jesse's voice asked softly in her ear. His face brushed warmly against hers, flooding her with reassurance and relief.

"How did you know it was me?" she whispered back.

"Are you kidding?" he asked, nuzzling closer. "Of *course* I knew. I'd know your voice anywhere."

She shuddered in his arms, unable to suppress a whimper. Then, to her surprise, she found herself blurting out a story she'd only ever shared with her diary.

"It's a nightmare I've had a bunch of times, but every time it's worse. My mom's coffin is in the ground, and I'm there by myself, trying to get her out. And then the dirt starts falling in, and it comes so fast it traps me. I yell and yell but no one comes. I know I'm going to be buried too, and then I am, and I can't breathe and—"

"All right. It's all right now," Jesse said, rocking her back and forth. "I can see why you woke up screaming. I thought *my* nightmares were bad!"

"You have nightmares too?" It was hard to imagine Jesse cowering under his blankets the way she did.

"Ever since I was ten. Sucks, doesn't it?"

"It really does," she said, relaxing into the safety of his arms.

The hubbub around the fire was dying down. Jenna moved from camper to camper, her long hair nearly brushing the ground as she bent to reassure each one. The adults had apparently decided there was no threat to the perimeter. Flashlights flipped out in rapid succession as one by one the kids were convinced to go back to sleep.

Jesse ran his fingers through Melanie's hair, raking it away from her face. "I love you," he whispered, kissing her cheek.

"I love you too."

It seemed impossible she had ever thought there

was anything about her that he wouldn't understand. They were connected somehow. Soul mates.

How could I have given Dan a second thought, when Jesse is everything I ever wanted? I was a fool to let Dan believe there was any sort of chance. Ever.

"What are you thinking about now?" Jesse whispered.

The camp had returned to darkness, an occasional rustling the only sign of life.

"Nothing important," she murmured, turning her lips up to his.

He kissed her softly, as if her recent frightening experience might have left her more delicate. Gentle little kisses brushed her cheekbones and eyelids, and traveled the bridge of her nose. She returned them across his straight brows, holding his face in both hands. And then her lips found his, and her heart swelled with relief.

Somehow she knew she wouldn't be having that nightmare again.

Fourteen

"Jenna! Come on out here!" Peter called, splashing water toward the shore from where he was swimming. "The water is really clear!"

All the campers, their counselors, and the other chaperones had hiked the short distance to a cove Miguel had found the evening before, lured by the promise of a clean sand beach. Now most of them were fooling around close to the shore, while David, Miguel, and Leah stood lifeguard duty. Jenna and Nicole had staked out a spot on the sand, neither one interested in getting wet.

"I just ate lunch," she called back "I'll get a stomachache."

"That's an old wives' tale," Melanie scoffed, running past with Jesse right on her heels. They dove into the water and splashed through the crowd, Melanie giggling the whole time. She was wearing a new bikini that made her look even sexier than usual, but Jenna was too depressed to care how her own suit compared.

"Come on!" Peter urged.

"Maybe later," she shouted.

Lisa plopped down in the sand beside Jenna and Nicole. "I don't want to go swimming either," she said, as if to contradict the pink bathing suit she wore. "Let's get all the girls who don't and play a game."

"What kind of game?" Nicole asked warily, obviously afraid that she might have to move. She didn't seem to have a lot more energy than Jenna did that Friday.

"Why don't you want to go swimming?" Jenna asked. "Most of the other kids are in the water."

Lisa put a hand to the ringlets she was so vain of. "I don't want to mess up my hair."

"Believe me," Jenna told her, "there's not a lot more damage you can do." The girl's curls were noticeably dusty and filled with bits of leaves from sleeping on the ground. "You'll have to shampoo when you get home anyway, so you might as well have fun."

"Then why aren't *you* swimming?" Lisa wanted to know.

"I just don't feel like it. Trust me, that's a whole different thing."

Lisa gave Jenna a suspicious look, then got up and went to join Belinda and another little girl playing in close to the shore.

"What are you doing tonight?" Nicole asked when they were alone again. "Anything good?"

Jenna pictured herself arriving home after being

181

gone two whole days, but it wasn't a pretty scene. Caitlin would be there, and they were barely even speaking after the fight they'd had about the wedding.

"Not really. You?" she asked Nicole.

Nicole sighed. "I have a date with Noel, but I wish it was tomorrow. I just don't feel . . . prepared."

"I know what you mean. It's going to take me a week to get this dirt out from under my nails."

"Yeah." Nicole looked off into space. "So, how are things going with Guy's band? Are you practicing tonight?"

"Not until Sunday night. To tell you the truth, I can use the break. This wedding's been driving me crazy."

Even as she said it, though, Jenna knew that wasn't exactly true. She'd been driving *herself* crazy. And now that she'd had some time to think, she realized that she'd been taking everyone else with her.

Cat never would have said that stuff to me if it wasn't true, she thought, blinking back the tears that threatened to fall despite Nicole's presence. *All I wanted was for her to have the best ever, most completely perfect wedding. How did things get so out of control? Even after Mom warned me, I didn't see what I was doing.*

The thought of sharing a room with Caitlin while her sister continued to give her the cold shoulder was making her completely miserable.

"Maybe I will go in the water," said Nicole, standing up so abruptly that a shower of sand rained down from her overalls.

Jenna brushed the grains from her face, barely noticing.

I have to apologize to Caitlin, she thought. *I'll apologize and offer to help her out with something she doesn't want to do. Something hard, like setting up all the tables and chairs at the reception. Oh! And I could be in charge of getting the tablecloths, and colored napkins, and those cute little skirts to put around the buffet tables. Maybe I could set the tables, too, with a vase of flowers for each one. Or place cards! I could make up a seating chart!*

For a moment her eyes widened with excitement. Then she shook her head. She was doing it again.

I have to apologize to Caitlin, she repeated firmly. *I'll apologize and promise to stay completely out of the wedding!*

"Ben! Your girlfriend's here!" Jason Fairchild teased as the Junior Explorers' bus rolled into the parking lot late Friday afternoon.

"Jason!" Ben protested.

"Yeah, Jason! Shut up!" Elton ordered. He obviously didn't want to be teased about a romance either, even if it was only his sister who was involved.

"Why don't you make me?" Jason invited.

But the bus doors were opening and Elton was able to clear out with dignity, something he did as quickly as possible. Ben, on the other hand, sat glued to his bench, wondering what to do, while everyone else clattered down the aisle and out onto the pavement. He had made up his mind to break things off with Bernie as soon as he got back from the overnight. He just hadn't expected it to be quite *this* soon.

Maybe she's only here for Elton again. If I just lay low for a while, maybe she'll take her brother and leave.

He watched as Bernie ran forward to meet Elton, slinging the boy's backpack over one of her shoulders and his sleeping bag over the other. She was wearing one of her loose gauze dresses, her arms bare and the hem of her skirt reaching almost to her ankles. Her light brown hair was moussed into smooth waves glittering with beaded bobby pins. She looked so sweet that for a moment his resolve almost failed him.

But only for a moment.

It's got to end sometime.

On the other hand, if he managed to hide out on the bus long enough, it didn't have to end right then.

The double back doors of the bus swung open, and Peter and David began handing belongings out into the waiting crowd.

"Ben!" Peter called. "What are you sitting there for? Come back and help us unload."

Ben cringed, then slowly, reluctantly, got up and walked down to the pavement. Kids and parents were milling about everywhere, loading up their waiting cars. Ben felt his hopes lift a bit as he lost himself in

184

the chaos. It was possible, if he could just sneak around to the—

"Ben!" Bernie called happily, waving both arms over her head. "Ben, over here!"

"Oh. Uh, hi, Bernie," he called lamely in return. Then, before she could move in his direction, he bolted around to the back of the bus, passing Maggie Conrad at one rear corner.

"Does Bernie Carter have a crush on you or something?" Maggie demanded.

Ben had seen Jenna's younger sister plenty over the past year, but they didn't typically converse. "Or something," he muttered, burying his head in the back of the bus and beginning to toss out sleeping bags.

"I don't blame you for ditching her!" Maggie said. "Who wants to be seen with such a nerd?"

"Exactly," Ben said savagely, hurling a bag out into the crowd.

"She was practically the biggest geek in our junior high school! Everybody teased her. Always glued to a computer, or reading some boring book. Not to mention that hippie fashion sense." Maggie shook her auburn curls. "I don't even know where she *gets* those clothes. Maybe they're her mother's."

Ben froze, the significance of her words coming through to him one syllable at a time. Had Maggie just said *Bernie* was the nerd?

"Bernie wasn't . . . popular?" he ventured.

185

"Puh-leese!" Maggie snorted. "*Popular?* She was barely even human."

"Maggie!" Mrs. Conrad scolded, walking up in time to overhear her daughter's last comment. "That's no way to talk about people."

"Sorry." But Maggie's eyes stayed fixed on Ben's, unrepentant.

"I thought you were getting Jenna's backpack for her so we can go," her mother added.

Through his confused haze, Ben slowly realized that the two of them had come to pick up Jenna and take her home. "Jenna's backpack?" he repeated. "I think I just saw that."

He fished it from the diminishing pile and handed it to Maggie.

"Good luck," she said with a meaningful roll of her eyes before her mother marched her off to the Conrads' station wagon.

Ben helped unload the rest of the bus mechanically, barely seeing what he was handing over. When the last sleeping bag had been disposed of, he sat heavily on the flat spot between the bus's open back doors, still reeling.

Bernie was the laughingstock of her junior high school? Was that even possible?

But she's so cute! his mind protested. *And so smart, and so sweet, and so nice!*

How could he be the only one to see that?

Junior high kids can be evil, he thought, remembering what a horror his own junior high experience had been. High school was much, much better. Maybe he was never going to be prom king, but hanging around with Eight Prime had at least gotten the bullies off his case. Not only that, but in the fall he would be a junior, which carried a certain status, if only because he'd survived. It was possible that to a freshman who didn't know any better, Ben might even look cool.

Wait a minute! A new thought sputtered through his brain like a string of firecrackers. *Is it possible that* Bernie *is lucky to get me?*

"We're going to the *lake?*" Nicole whined as Noel's sports car made the turn onto the familiar country road. "I just got *back* from the lake! You said we were going to a party."

"A party at the lake," he said, obviously pleased with himself. Now that she thought about it, Noel was always pleased with himself.

"But you told me to wear a dress!" she protested. "I'm going to freeze."

He cast a slightly annoyed look at her over the gearshift. "No, you aren't. It's perfectly warm outside. Besides, we're having a bonfire."

Oh, goody, Nicole thought, wishing he had let her in on his plan while there was still time to make an excuse. *It's the overnight all over again.*

She still hadn't gotten the woodsmoke out of her

pores from that other bonfire by the lake. Besides, if he had bothered to ask her, she'd have said she much preferred to be alone with him than lost in another crowd somewhere, barely able to talk to each other.

He hadn't asked her. He never did.

"All the guys are going to be there," Noel told her. "It ought to be a blast."

For you, Nicole thought sullenly.

But by the time Noel pulled into the gravel parking lot up at the lake, she was starting to think that the party might be all right after all. Someone was supposed to bring a sound system, and she could see the sparks from an enormous bonfire even before they got out of the car. Noel popped the lid on his tiny trunk and unwedged two lawn chairs, a blanket, and a cooler. Kicking off his shoes, he dropped them into the newly emptied space, advising her to do the same.

"Can you carry the cooler?" he asked, handing it over. "If you can, I can get the rest."

Judging by its weight, the cooler was obviously stuffed, but it was small enough that Nicole was able to carry it. They wandered downhill toward the fire, walking barefoot across first grass, then sand. The bonfire had been set midway down the gentle slope between the parking lot and the water, but it was far too large to be contained by one of the designated fire rings. Half-smashed wooden warehouse pallets had been tilted up against each other, forming a flaming cone. The blaze was so big that the lake picked up its reflection, a long streak of orange against the dark water. Fifty or more people already milled about on the sand surrounding the fire, swaying to the music, shouting over it, or just hanging around looking cool.

"The stars are out," Noel observed, setting their chairs down at the edge of the crowd.

They were, and Nicole wondered if they had been out the night before, too, when she'd been camping with the Junior Explorers. If so, she hadn't noticed. She was pretty sure she had never even looked up.

I've just been so on edge lately, so buried in my problems. . . .

Maybe Noel was a genius. Maybe a party was *exactly* what she needed.

I'd have died to get invited to a party like this last year. Especially with someone as cute as Noel.

Noel dropped into one of the chairs he had just set up and patted the seat of the other. "Take a load off," he instructed, beginning to root through the cooler he had placed on the sand between them. His hand came out with a tall dripping bottle that he handed to Nicole. "You like wine coolers, right?"

Nicole didn't recall that they had ever discussed her preferences in that regard, but she didn't want to hurt his feelings. She twisted off the cap and took a cautious sip. The drink was both bitter and too sweet, an overpowering fake fruit flavor apparently intended

189

to mask the alcohol. Nicole couldn't remember the last time she'd tasted something so vile.

"Blackberry," Noel told her, licking his lips after a long slug of his. "Pretty good, huh?"

She faked a smile, pretended to take another swallow, then propped her bottle up in the sand beside her chair. "Are we going to dance?" she asked, wanting to get closer to the action by the fire. Noel had them sitting practically in the dark.

"Yeah, later. When my crew gets here. There's no point to it now." He tossed back some more of his drink, apparently in a hurry to feel its effects.

"I hope you're not going to get drunk," said Nicole.

He raised his eyebrows at her.

"I mean, normally I wouldn't care," she added quickly, not wanting to seem uncool. "But that's a bad road home and you have to drive."

"I've had two sips," he complained. "I hope *you're* not going to be deadweight."

She drew in her breath, wounded. *What's that supposed to mean?* she wondered. *If he doesn't like the way I act, then why did he bring me? Or maybe . . . wait. Is that supposed to mean I'm fat?*

"Whoa! Look at Staci Stanley!" Noel exclaimed, pointing with his bottle. "She looks *hot!* I barely recognized her."

Nicole followed his gaze, eventually locating Staci near the fire. Nicole barely recognized her either. The girl had lost an impossible amount of weight. A short,

190

form-fitting spandex dress clung to skin that hugged bones almost as tightly. She was nothing but lines and angles, her jaw as sharp as a skeleton's.

"Is she . . . anorexic?" Nicole whispered, afraid to say the word at full volume.

"It's called dieting," Noel said. "Or have you forgotten?"

"Do you think I'm fat?" Nicole challenged. She had thought she looked pretty good that night, but Noel had never even mentioned her appearance.

"No," he admitted reluctantly. "Not *fat*. But look at Staci. I mean, if you looked like that . . . That's just *hot*," he said longingly.

"I think she looks a little sick." Nicole had always believed the old saying that it was impossible to be too rich or too thin, but now she wasn't so sure. Staci's hair hung limply on her back, and her eyes were sunk deep in their sockets.

"Rrrraaaaooooowww!" Noel made one hand into a cat claw and swiped it at Nicole. He laughed, and for a moment, Nicole nearly hated him.

"I'm not jealous," she said hotly. "I just can't believe you think that looks good."

Noel rolled his eyes and polished off his wine cooler. "Put it this way," he said, wiping his lips with the back of his hand. "No one is *ever* going to accuse Staci of being fat."

"And is that, like, the worst thing a person can be? Fat?"

He gave her a disbelieving look, then reached into the cooler and popped the lid off another bottle.

"Well, is it?" she demanded.

"Listen, Nicole, if you're trying to set me up for some sort of politically correct load of crap, then I'm not biting, all right? You know the score. Thin girls are just more popular."

He was right—she did know that. It was the reason she'd lost so much weight in the first place. So why did hearing him say it make her want to pull his perfectly spiked hair out by the roots?

"You're a double threat," he went on obliviously, "because you're thin *and* a cheerleader. You'd have to *really* screw up now, like drop the squad or gain fifty pounds or something, before people stopped liking you."

"If you—I—you—" she sputtered, the full impact of his words sinking in. "I have to go to the bathroom."

She jumped to her feet and started running without another word, not stopping until she reached the far side of the bathroom building, completely out of view. Leaning against the cold concrete wall, she hid her face and waited for the tears. Noel didn't like her—he was using her! He only wanted a thin cheerleader to show off to his friends.

She drew a shaky breath and screwed up her face, but her eyes remained stubbornly dry. Maybe she wasn't going to cry after all. As hard as she tried to focus on the outrage, all of a sudden she was seeing more clearly than she had in weeks.

And I only wanted to be a thin cheerleader in order to snag a cool guy like Noel. I don't really like him either.

Maybe there wasn't a problem, after all. They'd both gotten what they wanted.

Right?

Wrong. The tears came all at once, taking her by surprise. She *hadn't* only wanted to be thin, and popular, and dating the A list.

She had wanted someone to love her.

Fifteen

"I love you," Jesse told Melanie over the telephone. They were getting together later, doing the Saturday night thing, but for now they had to say good-bye.

"I love you more," she returned, ignoring the fact that Min had jumped onto the bedspread and begun attacking her toes.

"Good," he said with a laugh. "That's the way I like it."

After she got off the phone, though, Melanie started feeling nervous again. When she was talking to Jesse, it was easy to forget her problems. When she was by herself, all she could think about was Dan Meadows. And not in a good way either.

He's going to be here tomorrow, and what am I going to say to him? she worried. *How am I going to act?*

Picking up Min, she carried the kitten with her to the windows, burying tense fingers in fluffy white fur. She had pictured her next art lesson over and over again: Dan showing up, all cute . . . her complete disregard for his adorableness. She was pretty sure she could pull that off. After all, she had done it to Jesse for months.

And look how that turned out. Good plan, Andrews.

Ignoring Dan wasn't enough. She had to tell him to forget about anything happening between them. Ever.

That sounds like a fun conversation. Not to mention that I'm going to come off like the queen of ego. Maybe he doesn't even want me.

But he did. He had already made that pretty clear.

"Well, this bites," she told Min. "Let's hear your good ideas."

The kitten responded with one playful paw, tangling its claws in Melanie's hair.

"Ow!" Melanie freed herself and set Min on the floor, smiling as the kitten scampered under the bed, then stuck a paw back out to molest the fringe on the edge of the bedspread. Her smile didn't last very long.

Maybe I could talk to Dad.

Her father was working in his study again. From the hours he'd been keeping lately, no one would guess that his consulting job was supposed to be part time. Melanie had seen him take his first beer out of the fridge hours earlier, though, so there was nothing to say he was still accomplishing anything.

There's nothing to say he'll be in any condition to speak to me, either.

195

Besides, what would she tell him? That her big, bad art teacher was hitting on her? That she'd been leading him on? The whole situation was too embarrassing.

At last she moved to her bedroom door, shutting it behind her to keep the cat inside. Her bare feet scuffed across the second-story landing and down the marble stairs, one slow step at a time. Her father was still in his study, totally engrossed in writing something on a yellow legal pad, his single can of beer sweating, forgotten, on a coaster.

"You need a computer," Melanie ventured.

His head jerked up. She'd startled him.

"For what?" he asked.

"For whatever that is you're doing. That way, when you finished writing, it would already be typed, and you could check the spelling and everything."

He made a face. "They have people who type this stuff up at the office."

"*I* wouldn't mind having a computer. It would be a big help with my homework next year."

"Really?" Now he seemed interested. "How much do they cost?"

"Depends what you get. They're kind of like cars that way." She was speaking a language he understood; her father had once collected cars. "Speed adds cost. So do accessories."

"Well, there's no point buying a slow one," he said, exactly as she'd predicted.

"No. But if we got a good one, we could share it. Put it in the library or something."

"Yes. All right. You pick one out, and I'll go look at it." He returned to his writing, the subject settled.

"Um, okay." She leaned against his door frame, surprised by the unexpected turn the conversation had taken. She had come down to talk about Dan and had ended up with a computer. She was still standing there a minute later when her father looked up again.

"Is there something else you need?" he asked. "A car, maybe?"

"I do have a birthday coming up," she pointed out hopefully.

Her father snorted. "Right. Dream on."

"It's just . . . I kind of wanted to talk to you about my art lessons."

"Oh. Okay. How are those going?"

"Fine." She could have kicked herself for getting off to such a bad start. "I mean, um, I like *having* lessons. It's fun to learn more about painting."

"But?" he prompted, sensing something coming.

She took a deep breath. "I'm not sure Dan's the right teacher for me."

"You don't like him?"

"No, I do like him." *Too much. That's the problem.* "It's just . . . kind of awkward. Being all alone upstairs

197

with a guy I barely know. A *cute* guy. Who's always standing about an inch away . . ."

Mr. Andrews's eyes widened as if he hadn't considered that aspect of the situation. Judging by the way he was looking at her now, maybe he really hadn't.

"Did he . . ." Her father hesitated, obviously afraid to ask the question. "Did he do something?"

"No!" she exclaimed. "No, nothing like that, I swear. It's just . . . A woman teacher might be better, that's all."

"You run along," he told her, reaching for the telephone. "I'll take care of this."

"You're not going to get him in trouble, are you?" she asked anxiously.

"No. I'm just going to get him swapped for somebody else. These things happen. It's no big deal."

He was dialing before she was out of the room, Mr. Executive, back on his game.

I owe you one, Dad, she thought, creeping down the hall, through the kitchen, and out the back door.

Outside, the bright afternoon sun beat down on the pool and deck, glinting invitingly on crystal-clear water. Melanie took a deep breath of the summer air, the smell of freshly cut grass drifting to her over the fields. It was good to be alive on such a pretty day, with such a big weight off her shoulders. It was great to be alive to see her father's unexpected return from the dead. It was even better to be alive and in love. . . .

198

Melanie smiled.

It was just good to be alive.

"I can't believe you're already packing!" Peter said, walking into his brother's room and staring at the mess. The entire contents of David's closet seemed to be scattered across the floor. "The wedding isn't for another three weeks. What are you going to do? Live out of boxes?"

David laughed. "I'm not packing. I'm just trying to get this stuff sorted out."

"Then what are the boxes for?"

"The Salvation Army. Maybe they can use some of this stuff."

"Oh." Peter sat heavily on David's bed, hoping his mother wouldn't come down the hall and see what was going on. If it was depressing him, it would *definitely* depress her. "What are you giving them?"

"Clothes, mostly. Would you believe I still have clothes from high school in here? I'll never fit into these again. I don't know why Mom saved them."

Peter thought he knew, but he kept his mouth shut. He had promised, after all.

"You don't want any of this stuff, do you?" David asked suddenly. "I didn't even think of—"

"No. Well, maybe that jacket." Peter pointed to an old favorite of David's, something he'd seen his brother wear a thousand times.

"This thing?" David said dubiously, pulling it

out of the box he was kneeling beside. "It's pretty beat up, Peter."

"It'll be good for Saturdays at the park, when the weather turns cold again." He didn't want to admit that he'd probably just hang it in his closet as a reminder of the old days.

David nodded and tossed the coat across Peter's lap. "It ought to be all right for that. I don't think there's a lot more the Junior Explorers can do to it."

"You haven't been a counselor long enough, then." Peter laughed, but his heart wasn't really in it. It was sad to see David's room so torn apart, sad to realize that in a few more weeks it would be empty. . . .

It's not like he's been living in it so much lately, Peter reminded himself, trying to reason away his blues. For the last four years, David had been away at college, coming home only for holidays and vacations.

But it was different knowing that this time he wouldn't be coming back at all. He and Caitlin would stay for visits once they were married, but David would never live with them again.

"So. Got any plans for my old room yet?" David asked.

"What kind of plans?"

"I don't know," David said with a smile. "Maybe you're going to turn it into a weight room to pump up that scrawny physique of yours."

"Hey!" Peter protested. "I am not that skinny anymore! Not as skinny as I was, anyway."

"*Nobody's* that skinny," David teased, but Peter's mind was back on the original subject.

What *were* they going to do with David's room?

The answer slammed into his brain like a bolt of lightning. *Could we . . . ? Nah.*

But could *we?*

Peter jumped off David's bed and ran full speed down the hallway, surprising both his parents by bursting headlong into the den.

"What's the matter?" Mr. Altmann asked worriedly, putting down his paper. "You look—"

"Could *we* adopt Jason?" Peter blurted out. "David's room is going to be empty, and I'll help out like crazy, and I always kind of wanted a little brother, and, well . . . Could we?"

Mrs. Altmann put down her reading too, and exchanged a look with her husband. Peter heard David's footsteps coming down the hall behind him.

"He's really a good kid," Peter added intently. "I mean, he could be. If we just . . . Could we?"

All of a sudden, his parents broke into smiles, Mrs. Altmann with the bright sheen of tears behind hers. Standing up, she opened her arms wide to Peter.

"What took you so long?" she asked happily.

"You look handsome," Leah said, opening her front door to Miguel.

"You look hot." His eyes skimmed her pinned-up

201

hair and the slinky red dress she was wearing. "Are we going out? I thought we were eating here."

"We are," she said, taking him by the hand and pulling him inside. "But I wanted tonight to be special."

Inside the condominium, she had turned the lights down low again and put a romantic CD on the stereo. Candles glowed on the dinner table, which she had spent nearly an hour arranging with all the best china and crystal.

Miguel tilted his nose into the air and took a deep breath. "Smells good. When do we eat?"

"Is that all you can think about?" she asked, pretending to pout.

"It's probably all I *should* think about. . . ." One of his eyebrows climbed his forehead, making her laugh out loud.

"Come into the kitchen," she said, towing him along behind her. "You can see what I've got cooking."

She led him to the stove, where she lifted the lid on a pot of simmering spaghetti sauce. "I made it myself," she said proudly. "And salad, and French bread, and a chocolate cake for dessert."

"You made French bread?"

"Oh, all right," she admitted. "Technically, I bought the French bread. But I made the cake." She took the top off the cake server, eager for him to see her masterpiece.

"Sweet. But I see something sweeter."

He grabbed for her, pulling her into his arms and leaning back against the counter. "Let me show you what *I* cooked up for *you*," he said, bringing his lips down on hers.

Leah opened her mouth to his, melting up against him as she returned the kiss. Her hands raked through his dark hair and down his back. She could feel Miguel's muscles tense through his shirt everywhere she touched him. Her hands dropped lower and he groaned. It was amazing to have that kind of power over another person's body. Amazing. And not something to be taken lightly.

Miguel pulled away suddenly, breathing hard. "Just so I understand," he said. "This is as far as things are going tonight. Right?"

Leah gave him a crooked smile. "It's as far as they'll be going for quite a while."

"Then I think we'd better slow down." He pushed her gently back onto her own feet, putting a few inches between them.

"You're not upset, are you?" she asked worriedly. "I thought that was what you wanted too."

"I'm not upset." Taking her hands, he looked into her eyes. "I still want to marry you, Leah. And I want everything that goes with that. But whether it's now, or whether it's later . . ." He shrugged. "I want it to be right. And I want it *all* to be with no doubt."

She nodded, wondering what she had ever done to deserve such a wonderful boyfriend. She rested her head against his chest, so in love with him it hurt. "It will be," she whispered past the aching lump in her throat.

When she decided to give herself to Miguel, it would definitely be with no doubt. But for now she'd decided not to. Not because of her parents, and not because she was afraid of getting in trouble, but because over the past two weeks, she'd been forced to confront a lifetime of half-formed beliefs and assumptions and make a conscious choice. Not having sex now was *her* decision.

And waiting just felt right.

Sixteen

Jenna hung up her choir robe after Sunday morning services, in no real hurry to join her family. There was a coffee cake tasting in the church hall that morning, which meant that most of the congregation would be hanging around for at least an hour, tasting the various cakes and dessert bars that everyone had brought. Normally she loved stuff like that.

Normally Caitlin's speaking to me.

Jenna had apologized to her sister when she'd returned home from the overnight, and Caitlin had supposedly forgiven her, but things weren't the same between them. Caitlin had retreated into her old, shy shell, and Jenna was afraid to say anything more for fear of sounding bossy. All day Saturday they'd sidestepped each other, both desperate to keep the peace. At dinner, Mary Beth had brought up the reception, rubbing Jenna's nose in the fact that a place had been booked while she was camping. The Lakehouse Lodge, the swankiest place in Clearwater Crossing, had had a last-minute cancellation and the Conrads had jumped on it.

"You are *so* lucky," Mary Beth had told Caitlin, pointing with a breadstick. "I was sure you'd end up having your reception in the activities center at the park."

"I wasn't worried," Caitlin had said quietly. "Wherever we'd ended up would have been fine."

Jenna had silently picked peas out of her pasta, blinking back tears to think she'd missed the last major step in planning Caitlin's wedding. It would have been so fun to meet with the wedding consultant at the Lakehouse Lodge, to help choose the menu and decide how the tables would be arranged. Now she'd just have to see it all when she got there, like any other guest.

Stop moping and be glad for Caitlin! she ordered herself, the way she'd been doing all weekend. *Her wedding is sure to be great at the Lakehouse Lodge.*

Which only proved what Cat had said: She didn't need Jenna to help her.

Leaving the choir room, Jenna wandered reluctantly out to the courtyard. A few people were still outside, chatting in the morning sunshine, but most had already gone into the hall to check out the free food. Jenna started to go in too, but changed her mind in the doorway, heading instead for the wrought-iron bench she usually shared with Peter. He had called the day before, hinting that something big might be going on in his family, but he hadn't told her what yet. Maybe, if she waited, he'd come out and join her.

When someone finally did drop onto the bench beside her, though, it was Caitlin, not Peter.

"What are you doing out here?" she asked quietly. "We saved you some coffee cake."

"You did?" For once Jenna didn't feel like eating sweets.

"We thought you'd be right behind us."

"Oh."

For a moment they just sat there, looking at the ground. Then Caitlin's arm crept across Jenna's shoulders.

"I . . . I wanted to say that I'm sorry too," she whispered. "About snapping at you, I mean. I know you were trying to help."

"I really was," Jenna agreed miserably.

"And I wanted to ask you something. About the wedding."

Hope lifted Jenna's heart a little before she squashed it back down. *No matter what Caitlin asks me about the wedding, I'm not going to give an opinion. Even if it's killing me, I'm just going to say—*

"Would you be my maid of honor?"

"Wh-wh-what?"

Caitlin smiled. "It should probably be Mary Beth, since she's the oldest. But she won't care—and I know how much you do."

"I do! I *do* care," Jenna cried, forgetting to act cool. "Oh, Caitlin!"

"Is that a yes?"

"Yes?" Jenna echoed disbelievingly. "*Yes!* Of course!"

"And I was thinking, if you want, that we could change the color of your dress to blue. I know you like blue better."

"Really?" Jenna asked excitedly.

Blue was the color she had wanted in the first place! Not to mention how cool it would be to have a blue dress *now*, when all of her sisters were stuck wearing yellow. Except . . . Caitlin had a color scheme going, and one blue dress didn't exactly fit into it.

"But my dress won't match anything else," Jenna said.

Caitlin grinned. "It'll match your eyes."

For a moment Jenna grinned back, amazed that Caitlin was willing to do so much just to make her happy. Then she said what she should have said in the first place.

"Thanks, but I'd rather wear yellow. After all, it's *your* wedding, Caitlin."

"I have something to tell you," Ben informed Bernie solemnly. "I would have told you after the overnight Friday, but you took off so fast I couldn't find you."

"I, uh . . . I remembered I had something important to do," Bernie said vaguely, looking over his head in the direction of the kitchen.

They were sitting on opposite sides of a tiny back table in Slice of Rome, and the crowd was lighter than usual that night, giving them plenty of privacy. Ben had been so busy planning the speech he was about to make that he had barely talked during dinner, leaving Bernie to comment on the pizza and the special pistachio ice cream the restaurant only served on Sundays.

"Well, this is important too," Ben said, reaching for one of her hands across the empty tabletop.

Bernie jerked them into her lap. "Let's go outside," she said. "I don't want to have this discussion in here."

"You don't even know what I'm going to say!" he protested.

"Whatever it is, I'd rather hear it outside."

She rose abruptly, cutting off further argument, and Ben had no choice but to leave a quick tip and follow her to the cash register. He tried not to panic as he paid for their dinner—he could say what he needed to outside as well as in—but after all the visualization he'd done to work himself up to this moment, he was definitely flustered by the sudden change of venue. He walked Bernie out to the parking lot, trying to regroup.

"It's nice out tonight," he said, feeling the need to

work up to his real subject again. "Still so warm and—"

"Look, Ben," Bernie interrupted, a quiver in her voice. "I know what you're going to say, so just say it."

"What?" he said, taken aback. He had never seen Bernie so upset. Not only was her voice all wobbly, but her cheeks had flushed red and her eyes were suddenly full of tears.

"I saw you talking to Maggie Conrad. I may be a geek, but I'm not a fool. You're going to break up with me now, so hurry up and do it!"

"What? No! You've got it all wrong," he told her. "I was going to break up with you *before* I talked to Maggie, but now everything's good again."

Bernie looked dumbfounded. "She didn't tell you that ... um ... that in junior high I wasn't very, um ..."

Ben grabbed both her hands. "No, she *did* tell me," he corrected. "And it was the best news I ever got."

Bernie simply stared. He obviously wasn't making sense, and in the excitement he'd totally forgotten his prepared speech.

"I have a confession to make," he told her. "I'm not as cool as you think I am. I was a total reject in junior high, and the first year and a half of high school weren't too great either. Maggie said you were a computer geek. Well, you can't even mention my name in the same *sentence* with computers around CCHS, unless you want to start a riot."

"Why?" she asked breathlessly, as if still not sure whether to believe him.

"Little programming problem involving crashing a whole lot of student hard drives," he admitted sheepishly. "The only reason people didn't kill me is that I'm friends with the rest of Eight Prime. Miguel, and Jesse, and Melanie . . . those are some of the most popular people in school."

"Well, but you're cool *now*," she insisted.

Ben shook his head. "Not only am I a geek, I'm the son of two even bigger geeks. My case is probably hopeless."

"I have to wear my mother's hand-me-downs." She said it like a challenge.

"Mitch Powell calls me Pimple." He squeezed her hands, desperate for her to understand. "But the thing is, I don't care when I'm with you. I mean, I know I'm not cool, but you make me feel like I am. Do you know what I mean?"

"Yes," she said slowly. "I never thought I was pretty, or even average-looking, before. And then I saw the way you look at me . . ."

Later Ben would marvel at what had possessed him, but in that moment he knew exactly what to do. Pulling Bernie forward, he brought his lips to hers as if he'd been kissing girls all his life. She went a bit stiff at first, taken by surprise, but by the time their mouths parted again, they both knew it didn't matter what anyone else thought of them.

"You are beautiful," he told her.

Nicole drove slowly down the quiet street, wondering if she was having some sort of nervous breakdown. That was the only explanation she could come up with for cruising Guy's neighborhood on a Sunday night, sneaking up on his house under cover of darkness. A half block away she cut her engine and headlights and rolled the final distance to the stretch of curb outside his garage, grateful to see that the door was down. If her approach had been silent enough, no one would ever guess she was there.

Slowly, carefully, Nicole let down the car window. Rock music filled the air outside, drifting in with the nighttime breeze. Sighing with relief, she slouched low in the seat, secure in the knowledge that no one had heard her pull up. Trinity was practicing, just as Jenna had said they would be. Nicole had come to listen.

Not that they probably wouldn't let me in if I just knocked on the door.

Not that I'd ever do that.

There was too much past history between her and Guy to try to pretend she had just dropped by. *Why* had she dropped by? That's what he would want to know.

Nicole wouldn't have minded knowing that herself.

I just want to hear how they sound now, that's all.

She tried to concentrate on the music. Guy's voice was as strong and sure as ever, singing lyrics to a song Nicole hadn't heard before. Jenna contributed harmonies, her voice blending so perfectly with his that Nicole's mood sank even lower.

If I could have accompanied him like that, maybe we'd still be together.

Not that they'd ever made such a great couple. She and Guy had argued more than anything, unable to agree on the simplest subjects. If he had just been willing to bend a little more . . .

Or if she had.

Well, it's over now.

Besides, she and Noel had ended up having a pretty good time together at the party Friday night. Once she'd gotten over her little crying jag, she'd managed to suck down a couple of those disgusting wine coolers and they had danced and made out most of the rest of the night. The key had been to adjust her expectations. She understood what kind of relationship they had now. Noel wasn't going to dump her. Not unless he found someone who could do even more for his image.

And I don't really care if he does.

The music stopped, then started up again. Guy began singing the song he had won the battle of the bands contest with at the Hearts for God rally in Los Angeles. Nicole closed her eyes, remembering.

213

All the girls in the audience had been beside themselves, envying her for knowing him. Nicole had mostly been embarrassed. Embarrassed that he would sing such Christian lyrics, embarrassed that he would sing them in such public places. It wasn't that she didn't believe what he was singing . . . she just had trouble saying it out loud sometimes.

But Guy was never ashamed. He said what he believed. He never compromised just because it was more convenient.

"Let's do the wedding song," Jenna said when Guy's song came to a close. The band started playing something slow.

"*Now and always,*" Jenna came in, her voice so full and gorgeous it could shatter a person like crystal.

Guy picked up the harmony. "*Love is patient, love is kind. It always protects, always trusts, always perseveres.*"

Hot tears squeezed from beneath Nicole's lashes. She didn't know why she was crying.

She still didn't even know why she was there.

Find out what happens next in the series finale, Clearwater Crossing #20, *Don't Look Back.*

About the Author

Laura Peyton Roberts is the author of numerous books for young readers, including all the titles in the Clearwater Crossing series. She holds degrees in both English and geology from San Diego State University. A native Californian, Laura lives in San Diego with her husband and two dogs.

Don't Look Back

The members of Eight Prime have been through a year full of ups and downs, but now summer is ending, and so is their time together. . . .

Leah and Miguel are getting ready to start college apart, and Peter's already feeling the pressure of senior year. Jenna can't believe she's going to be the oldest sister in the Conrad house now that Caitlin's marrying David. Meanwhile, Ben's still in starry-eyed shock over the fact that he has a girlfriend, Melanie and Jesse will be starting the new school year as a couple, and Nicole is starting to wonder if couplehood is all it's cracked up to be!

None of them can be sure what the coming year will bring. But they still have these last few days of summer. . . .

Don't miss the Clearwater Crossing series finale, coming in November 2001!